TWIST OF FATE

No Turning Back

E.A. Kellner

Acknowledgments

My parents passed away years ago, but their influence lives on in this book. My Mother was a writer and constantly supported my efforts to write. My Dad was a schmoozer and left me the gift of gab.

I was the Sports Editor of *The Brown & Gold* newspaper for Haverhill High School. My mentor, George Merrill gave me endless guidance and support. He left the school, and I received a telegram from Stratford-on-the-Avon in England from Mr. Merrill. He wrote: "You have a gift of writing. You will go far in this field. Good luck."

I want to thank Victoria Valentine, the publisher of *Skyline Magazine*, who helped me to submit my interview with Gary Wolf, the creator of *Roger Rabbit*.

I would like to thank Mr. Wolf for his most interesting interview. I had to submit my questions to him prior to his interview. He said he would give me one hour, and the interview lasted almost two hours. He was impressed with my research.

Way back when I was asked to write an interview with the Massachusetts Boxing Commissioner, the interview went well, and he gave me a press pass to watch fights at Boston Garden and I sat ringside. I was so close to the action that one of the boxers took a hard right and he bled across my notes.

Thank you also go to Bill Nichols, publisher of *Planet North Shore*, who gave me a column that lasted two years: "Disability and You: Everything You Always Wanted to Ask."

Thanks go to the leader of a feminine creative writing course. When I walked through the door, she said, "What are you doing here? I responded with, "I want to learn how to write." I attended the group with my mother. We formed a writing group after the course, and this was where *Sidney the Uncommon Squirrel* was born. We met monthly for two years.

I am very grateful for the clients of Eliot Community Human Services of the Gloucester office who worked with me for seven years to produce some wonderful writing. This writing group was one of the most popular groups whose members rarely missed a meeting. They poured their hearts out and honestly shared their feelings as folks with chronic mental health problems.

I would like to thank the Carolina Forest Authors Club for their support and critique of this book. Their input was invaluable. They provided a safe place to write. A safe place to critique each other's works. It is a 'No Judgment Zone.' The group continues to meet twice a month through zoom and the Carolina Forest Library.

Thanks go to Karon Millonzi for your meticulous review of this book. You have a very sharp eye for corrections and additions.

Oh Vicki, my sister, you surprised me with your review. You were spot on with your review and your love for me. I will forever love you to bits.

My heart goes out to my editor, Jessica Tilles, Owner/ Creative Director of TWA Solutions & Services. Jessica held my hand and walked me through the publishing process.

Finally, thanks to my wife, Alice, for her thorough review of this book and her unconditional support. She continued to gently push me to write. "Do what you want to do." I'd like to thank her for her love and tolerance of my many hours sitting in front of the computer.

State of Illinois General Laws – Part IV – Title II – Chapter 278

Section 4. The following oath shall be administered to the jurors for the trial of all criminal cases which are not capital:

The following oath shall be administered to the jurors for the trial of capital cases:

You shall well and truly try, and true deliverance make, between the state and the prisoner at the bar, whom you shall have in charge, according to your evidence; so, help you God.

"One 44, two 45 Charlotte" by NAS

"Let the trigger blow, seven shots now he is laying on the ground blood on the floor then we shot some more."

Chapter One

April 24, 1994, 8:00 p.m.

Grasping the back of her head, as it moved in sync with his hips, D'Quandree Jones tossed his head back and moaned. "Hey, baby, suck me hard, suck me dry, bitch." The love couple moved to the music of N.W.A.'s, "Fuck the Police."

Breathing fast, Anodiwa anticipated the yummy load heading her way. She felt the rush in Jones's penis and shivered as the massive ejection erupted and sent man-gravy all over her face, dripping down to her undulating breasts.

Just then, someone yelled from the other room. "Hey, Ree, the fucking phone call you been waiting for is here."

Jones pushed the Black beauty to one side of the bed and slid across the purple satin sheets to take the phone call.

Snake Eyes reported, "The muthafucka will be at the West End Park at ten o'clock tonight."

"Good. You make sure the muthafucka is there and don't fuck this up or else your ass is mine."

"Don't worry, Ree, he'll be there."

The hot lovers had the whole second floor to themselves. A king-sized bed with gold lights on each night table. A twenty-one-year-old natural beauty and runner-up in this year's beauty contest in Zimbabwe, Anodiwa Tshuma came to this country last month and became Jones's girlfriend right out of the gate. She was statuesque at five-foot-ten, breathtaking in a black bikini, and she spoke impeccable English.

Jones looked back at his woman. "Boo, let me settle over your mound of wetness and lick and drink your warm liquid and just forget about every other fuckin' thing going down."

"Come on, baby, you know what I like. I have nothing but a fuckin' fire waiting to be doused."

Jones settled on her wetness and dug his tongue as far as it could go. He felt the warm liquid on his face and couldn't stop licking. He then sat up and turned her on her back and entered no-man's-land in her anus. Anodiwa groaned with each plunge of his penis. Jones climaxed, and the two lay back in bed sweating, and he thought, *This ain't shit like the Stones' hit, "I Can't Get No Satisfaction."*

Jones was pumped and looked forward to snuffing the Attorney General's only witness to his carjacking case. *That muthafuckin' Alphonse Ferguson Attorney General will go down in flames when those fucking charges against me are dropped*, he thought.

Jumping into the shower, Jones felt relieved that the carjacking charges would soon disappear. He didn't like the idea of being convicted of aggravated carjacking, which carried a sentence of up to twenty years with a five-year minimum sentence in Illinois.

Jones began washing his hair and his head. He slowly moved down his chest and flexed his muscles as he cleaned both arms. He felt the strength that brought him to the top of the heap. He held his package and was proud of the length of his tool, which brought pleasure to many women. He carefully moved down between his legs. He sat down on the shower stool to wash his legs and feet.

Walking out of the bathroom and into his bedroom, Jones stood still and looked around. He thought, *I'm doing okay*. He was happy that he recently upgraded his bedroom, complete with a purple theme from the tray ceiling to the purple blanket, sheets and pillows to the purple canopy draping the bed. The bedroom floor was elevated with three very wide steps and wrought iron fencing going up the stairs. Finally, there were five cylindrical columns surrounding the bed.

The twenty-nine-year-old gangbanger descended the circular staircase with an air of confidence as he entered the living room wearing black pants, a black shirt, and a black hoodie, the color of the Parker Street Posse. He grabbed a chicken leg and, in between bites, ordered four men to come with him that night.

"We are going to blast that motherfuckin' snitch and there will be nothing left of him," bellowed Jones. "I am not going to waste away in prison for twenty years for this muthafucka. I need to snuff Jenkins tonight and free myself from Mr. Law Man."

Jones devoured chicken so fast even Colonel Sanders couldn't keep up with the demands of the brothers preparing for one of their favorite moments, "quieting a snitch."

D'Quandree Jones rose to the top in the Parker Street Posse and quickly gained the attention of the Anti-Crime Unit spearheaded by Attorney General Alphonse Ferguson. Ferguson's success with gang prosecutions worried Jones, and he knew he had to blast the snitch's brain matter into the next century.

Jones mainly dealt with drugs, but did not stop there. He led home invasions, stole cars, and other mayhem. He has been successful with his law-breaking activities and now must deal with Attorney General Ferguson.

Standing six-foot-five and weighing two hundred fifty pounds, Jones' muscular arms and legs presented an intimidating force that terrified all who tried his patience. Gang symbols that included a devil spitting out fire and blood covered his arms. The word "hate" covered his bald head. His rules are simple: *"Do what he says. Stand in his way and you will reach the pearly gates and you will meet St. Peter sooner than you planned."*

Jones grew up in poverty and he swore he would climb his way out of this way of life, and he would get money anyway he could. A life of crime was not out of the question.

He was a thief from an early age, and he began stealing lunch money from the other students. It was not long before he had his own corner, pushing drugs for local gangs.

He was always taller than other kids his own age and he could buy liquor as a teen. His street cred increased as he moved from weed to cocaine.

The gang occupied a Painted Lady given to Jones from Crip, making good on a promise. The Crip gunned down three of Jones's men for no reason, and thus the deliverance of the deed to Jones. The gang lair became a scene of brothers arming themselves with Ultra-Compact 45 Auto P239 and Barretta AR 70/223 assault rifles with extra clips in their jackets.

"Yeah, Ree, let's fill that punk ass full of lead," said Snake Eyes.

The restored Painted Lady had yellow and red trim, blue siding, and a red metallic roof. Pansies, the annual plants for the flower beds in the front of the house, added fragrance and color to the garden landscape. It was an oxymoron that serious criminal activity existed within the walls of this building.

"Who is going to ride with who?" asked Deshaun.

"Deshaun, you will go with me and Frankie. Lucky and Washington will ride together, and Snake Eyes will pick up Jenkins," said D'Quandree.

"It will be good to see Ree free from the chase of fuckin' Attorney General Ferguson," shared Snake Eyes. "The Boss has seen nothing but all these cops after him for years. I look forward to releasing the Boss from the yoke of the Law Man. Let's get that snitch, Jenkins."

"You got that fuckin' right," added Washington. "Let's plug that shit full of lead tonight.

Chapter Two

April 24, 1994, 7:00 a.m.

There was a light rain outside, and Deon Jenkins could not get to sleep. He hadn't been able to sleep since the carjacking and the trial of D'Quandree Jones. He often thought that maybe he was in the wrong fucking place at the wrong fucking time. *I know, I'll tell D'Quandree that I will state that I don't know who stole that car at the trial. It was dark and I couldn't see his face. Yeah, that's what I'm going to do. I gotta make things right with him.*

The gang had ostracized him and he tried to survive one day at a time with his wife, Ya'Lika, and their three children. He worked at Frank's Auto Service, changing tires and aligning front ends for ten years, and received a few pay raises, which enabled him to have a roof over their heads and a place they could call home.

Deon Jenkins was a typical African American male often described by victims of crime. He was in his late twenties, with an average height and average weight. He had gang tattoos over both arms, PSP Parker Street Posse, led by Jones. However, since he witnessed the carjacking, gang members had constantly harassed him.

Ya'Lika was making breakfast for the children, as Deon was getting dressed for his workday. They lived in a small two-bedroom house with one bathroom. They had practically no closet space and there were clothes all over the place, not to mention all the toys.

Ya'Lika was afraid for his life. "Deon, you don't have to go through with the trial. You could say, 'I don't remember,' when asked about the carjacking. Don't be a fuckin' hero. We need you. I need you. I don't know what I would do without you. I left high school in the tenth grade. I have no work skills. I have to take care of the children and childcare is so expensive."

"Don't worry, honey, I'll be okay. Jones has enough trouble as it is and doesn't want a murder on his hands. I gotta do what is right." He tore apart the last pork chop. He burped and smiled as he put her hand in his.

"I worry, that is all. I don't want you to be dead, right. I need you."

Deon reached for his coffee and bagged lunch and went to work as usual.

At work, Deon got his assignments from the lead mechanic and began his first tire change for a 1995 Chevy

Silverado. He got the truck on the lift and began changing the old tires and replacing them with K1500 Silverado regular cab tires.

Talking to himself, Deon attempted to analyze the issue. "Okay, if the original tires did not show any unusual wear and your car isn't pulling or drifting, then your alignment should be fine with your new tires. We rarely have an alignment done unless I replace any steering or suspension component that affects the toe or caster angles, camber I can adjust with my special level. Is that a bad thing? I don't really think so. It's worked for me for years. Is that the best practice? Maybe not. But if you read your tires, they'll tell you if there is a major problem."

He worked on another couple of cars, and it was time for lunch. There was a small dirty lunchroom in the garage and Deon ate his lunch there. He had a ham sandwich with chips. The other mechanics joined him, and they ate, complaining about their bills and the end of the Major League Baseball strike.

"Those bastards make more money than anyone and they are striking for more," said Frankie.

"You got that right. The muthafuckas are greedy," added Tony.

"Well, we can't do anything about it, but complain," said Deon.

"You always gotta take the middle road. The fuckin' players make more than God. They are greedy and we must sit here and work our asses off just to have a roof above our families. It sucks," ended Frankie.

"Time to get back to work."

Jenkins completed his workday, and he headed home. He liked working at Frank's. It was only ten miles from his house. He opened the front door to the aroma of his favorite meal: fried catfish, mac n cheese, and black-eyed peas with cornbread. He read the package the fish came in and it read: *This gives further proof to the old saying, 'Fish should swim twice—once in water and once in grease.*

He gave his wife a hug and a kiss and asked her, "How was your day?" as he sat at the dinner table.

"Not good," she replied. "I can't stop worrying about you. You say things are going to be okay, but I don't trust that fuckin' Jones."

They were startled by the phone ringing, and Deon picked it up.

"We are getting together tonight to plan how we are going to deal with the fuckin' Attorney General Ferguson," said Snake Eyes. "I'll pick you up at nine-thirty and we are meeting at West End Park."

"Okay, I'll be ready." He hung up the phone.

"Who was that, honey?" asked Ya'Lika.

"Snake Eyes called to let me know that the guys are getting together to make plans about what to do with that muthafucka, Attorney General Ferguson."

"I don't like this. Are you sure you have to go?"

"I'm there. There will be no more discussion."

Chapter Three

April 24, 1994, 9:30 p.m.

The drive to the park would only take fifteen minutes, and Jones wanted to arrive early to set the stage for his attempt to free himself from the arms of Attorney General Alphonse Ferguson. The rain cleared hours ago, but the night smelled like danger.

"So, what is the plan? asked Jenkins.

"I don't know. Let's wait to see what Ree has to say," replied Snake Eyes.

As they piled out of the 1995 Mercedes-Benz S 420, Jones demanded that they better aim to kill.

"Motherfucking Jenkins will wish he never offered to side with the lawman," Jones told the gangsters as he positioned his men. Frankie, go behind that fucking red Ford. Lucky, stay with me, and Deshaun, go behind that fucking tool shed with Washington. We are early and ready," D'Quandree said to his boys.

At exactly 10:00 p.m., a 1995 Mustang GT 5.0 slowly made its way to the designated location for the nocturnal rendezvous driven by Snake Eye.

Simultaneously, Jenkins arrived at the park at 10:00 p.m., looked out the window, and saw familiar sights as they sped through the streets. *Will this be the last time I can see these neighborhoods? It is strange to meet at a park to do gang planning. Will this truly be the end of my life? Is this what my wife was afraid might happen? We are at the park, and I cannot see anyone.*

Jenkins got out of his car and followed Snake Eyes to the bench. He saw D'Quandree Jones and the rest of the gang armed and he thought, *This is it. This is what my wife warned me about. I am going to be killed right here. Fuck!*

"Yo, Jenkins! Muthafucka, why did you inform the AG that you saw me stealing that car? Why didn't you keep your motherfucking trap shut? You left me with no choice, and I have to blast your ass!" yelled Jones.

"Wait a minute! I have a wife and three children. Yeah, I fucked up when I went to the cops, but I needed money, and you didn't include me in your muthafuckin' game. I just needed some money. You can understand that, can't you?"

"You piss me the fuck off!" Jones opened fire on Jenkins and his body bounced left and right as each bullet hit him, causing him to slump to the ground. Jenkins and the bench were drenched in blood.

"Okay, wrap the muthafucka in plastic and shove him in your trunk. Dump the muthafucka in the woods outside of town," added Jones.

Jones drove back to his apartment alone. He smiled and thought, *This fucking town is mine and it has been white for too long.* Overton is the third largest city in Illinois, and he owned that town.

D'Quandree Jones returned home and Anodiwa opened the door wearing nothing but red CFM shoes. She put her arms around him and softly said, "I missed you, baby. I'm glad you're home. I'll make a nice drink for you, and we'll take a nice hot bath together."

Jones smiled and hugged his girl. "That sounds like a great idea. Let's do it."

He felt relieved that the charges would disappear. Now he could get back to life as he knew it. He smiled as he thought he was one step ahead of the law and had managed to earn a small fortune in drugs and stolen cars.

Anodiwa waited for him in the hot bubble bath, surrounded by candles. He slid right into her slick, soapy pleasure ditch. She moaned as he ran his fingers all over her body, paying special attention to her pussy. She mounted and moved seductively up and down, guiding his huge cock between her legs. They moved in unison and soon climaxed as she disappeared into his arms. They lay drinking wine, contented and comfortable until the water cooled.

Chapter Four

April 25, 1994, Across Town, 6:00 a.m.

The alarm rang at 6:00 a.m., announcing the beginning of another day as the blond-haired beauty stretched, shut the alarm, slowly pushed the bedcovers, and sat up on the edge of the bed. Charlotte Steele wiped the night from her eyes and made her way to the en suite to prepare for a new day.

The sun was creeping through the shades. She struggled to keep her eyes open as she thought about last night and the good time she had with her fiancé, Connor Ellis. However, she knew that she had to say something to him about ending their relationship. She travels a lot and didn't feel comfortable leaving him all the time. Teeth brushed, and mouth gargled, she started the shower and began to wake up as the water cascaded down her seductive body.

Charlotte was good-looking enough not to need any further enhancements. She was a burst of energy at five-foot-five. The world was a feast for all eyes, and the ways a woman can be beautiful are truly too many to count. But yeah, yellow-haired, blue-eyed beauty. Even the words alone make a man feel a bit tingly.

A look in her blue eyes showed she was sincere and kind. She had tattoos on her right arm that resembled the phases of the moon running down the back of her arm to just below her shoulder from her elbow.

As she looked in the mirror applying her black eyeliner, she was pleased with her hair parted to the right and a light dab of red lipstick, which was empowering. A woman dressing her lips in red will draw attention to her, especially her mouth, and, subsequently, the words that come out of it. "It's a symbol of prowess," some would say.

As a freelance writer/photographer, she traveled the world to cover crises, wars, and important issues du jour. She was looking forward to writing her feature piece for *National Geographic* with her interview with Bill Wilson, Deputy Assistant Director for Fish and Wildlife Alaska region, and co-chair of a paper that warned: "As the Arctic warms faster than any other place on the planet and sea ice declines, there is only one sure way to save polar bears from extinction and that is the reduction of human emission of greenhouse gases into the atmosphere. Short of action that effectively addresses the primary of diminishing sea ice, the agency's plan said, "it is unlikely polar bears will survive."

Charlotte was pleased that her piece for *National Geographic* was completed and ready for submission. She felt very grateful she had a career she thoroughly enjoyed and assignments that took her all over the world.

At the same time, she lamented that she would not be able to marry Connor. She never knew where her next assignment would take her, nor how long she would remain at the specified site to do her research and writing.

Widely respected for her ability to provide truthful and dynamic writing, Charlotte was in high demand and had a waiting list of articles that required her attention to detail and fact. *The Washington Post*, *The New York Times*, CNN, MSNBC, BBC and many other news outlets had her on speed dial.

Extremely tired after a day of writing, she finished a glass of her favorite white wine, Domaine Ramonet Montrachet Grand Cru, which demanded a price of $1,257 a bottle. Aside from the aroma and taste of fine Chardonnay Grapes, this white wine brand also boasted rich lemon notes and a citrus palate. She realized she had expensive taste in wine but smiled and thought she was worth it.

Her eyes became very heavy, and she hugged her pillow around two o'clock in the morning and fell asleep.

Chapter Five

April 26, 1994, Jury Service, Tuesday Morning Mail
Charlotte retrieved the morning mail and received a summons for Jury Duty from the Circuit Court of Cook County. She felt this could be interesting, and thought, *I might serve a couple of days, or I might end up on a murder trial that could go on for weeks. I don't know. Wait a minute, I have my own business. How will I get paid? The court will pay for my first three days, but I own my own business. I just started it and how can I pay myself? Thoughts for another day.*

Of course, the freelance writer discussed this notice with friends and family. The stories varied greatly. Her sister, Tina, served a week on a civil disturbance trial. Her uncle, Larry, didn't serve at all. He showed up at the predetermined time and, by noon, he was excused along with the other jurors since there wasn't a trial that required a sitting jury.

She went about her business and didn't give this summons another thought until she got close to her service date. She would have to make sure that she would meet all her deadlines, but there were always evenings and weekends for this work.

Charlotte realized she had to see Connor one more time and let him know she could no longer see him. She did not have a normal life and was always on the go. She couldn't stop to recognize her feelings. She and Connor had been a couple for five years. Suddenly, she put the brakes on long enough to experience an overwhelming desire to bawl like a baby. She didn't realize the void she would create by saying goodbye to Connor. She wiped her eyes and dialed Connor's number.

"Hi, Connor. I'd like to see you tonight. Maybe we could have dinner together."

"Sounds good to me. I had a good time last night. Where do you want to go?"

"How about Miller's Pub? I can meet you there at six o'clock."

"Okay. I'll meet you there."

Charlotte knew she had to see Connor one more time. She had known this for some time, but for one reason or another, she was not honest with him about ending their relationship. She loved him, but she didn't want to lead him on anymore and wanted to set things right. Even though he was a port in the storm every time she returned home, she still had feelings for him. She could interview leaders around the globe with ease, but realized why it had taken her so long to face him with the truth. Tears started rolling down her cheeks and she had difficulty dealing with this emotion.

Around four o'clock, she got ready for her meeting with Connor. She was not the one to get emotional. It would take her a half hour to drive to the restaurant. She wore jeans and a red Halogen Lace & Crepe top. She didn't need a jacket. It was eight-six degrees and mostly cloudy.

She arrived at the Pub and met Connor. He had short, tousled hair with jeans and a blue denim shirt, and white high-top sneakers. The hostess led them to a table, and they ordered wine. The regular dinner crowd was shouting conversations and laughing, and the sound system played Jewel's "Who Will Save Your Soul."

They hugged, and sat at their table. Connor asked, "So, how was your day today?"

"I had a good day. Got some work done. I received a notice that I may have to have jury duty. Have you ever served on a jury?"

"No. Not yet."

"Well, I'll have to wait and see. So, I wanted to meet with you to let you know that we can no longer be a couple. This is very difficult for me. I love you very much, but I have to let you go. I can no longer be with you. I'm breaking our engagement." She took off the engagement ring and handed it to Connor.

"What are you talking about? We had a great time last night."

"I know, but I have been thinking about this for a while. We cannot go on. I don't think it is fair for you to have to wait for me while I travel and work all over the globe. It is very difficult to think of marriage with you. You deserve to meet someone who you can call and make plans for dinner or a movie or not have to wait weeks for me to return. I love you, but I think it is best that we call it quits."

"What are you saying? I love you. Yes, I miss you when you are away on an assignment." Connor was stunned as he tried to hide the tears welling in his eyes. "What are you saying?"

"It is better that we no longer see each other. It is time to say goodbye."

"I'm totally confused. Everything has been perfect up to now."

"I know, but it must end. This is so difficult for me." She spoke between sobs.

"Do you want some time to think this over?"

"I've been thinking about this for some time, and I didn't know what to say to you."

"Why didn't you say something before tonight? Why keep me in the dark?"

"I have a lot on my plate and a relationship or future with you is no longer a plan for me."

"If that is what you want?" Connor got up from the table.

"It is."

"Well, there is no reason for me to hang around. I love you and have a good life."

Before leaving the restaurant, Connor stopped, turned around, and gave Charlotte a dirty look.

The waitress came to the table and asked if she wanted anything else.

"Please get me the check. I lost my appetite."

Charlotte paid the check and walked for a while before she got into her car. She felt good that she finally made a move from her relationship with Connor. She loved him, but she fell out of love. They were engaged for two years. She found it very difficult to juggle her life and make room for Connor. She sat looking at the traffic and wished she had not waited so long to end the affair. She knew she had a lot on her plate, and she had to concentrate on her work. She put the car into drive and began her short ride home.

Chapter Six

April 26, 1994, Midnight —Where's My Husband?

Ya'lika Jenkins was feeling very nervous that her husband was not home. She called family members, asking if anyone had seen Deon. No one saw him.

She decided to call D'Quandree Jones to see if he knew anything about the whereabouts of her husband.

"Hi, may I speak with Mr. Jones?"

"Hi, this is D'Quandree Jones, may I help you?"

"Mr. Jones, my husband, Deon Jenkins, left the house about nine-thirty to meet with you. Do you know where he is?"

"Well, we did meet with him and then we went home, and I was led to believe that he returned home. You haven't seen him? I don't know what to say. He isn't here."

"Are you sure he left to return home?"

"As I said, our meeting was over, and we all left the park to go home. I don't know what happened to him. If I see him, I will surely tell him that you are looking for him."

"Thank you, Mr. Jones."

Ya'Lika was still upset. She called the police and spoke with Detective Jerry Polansky. "My husband, Deon Jenkins, left the house tonight around nine-thirty and did not return home. I'm worried about him. Have you heard anything about him?"

"Who is this calling?"

"My name is Ya'Lika Jenkins, and I am his wife."

"Well, ma'am, have you checked with his friends and relatives? Maybe he met up with some friends and is hanging out with them."

"I told him not to go out. I told him to stay home. I was very worried. He had a meeting with D'Quandree Jones and others. I told him not to be a martyr. He was an eyewitness to an alleged carjacking by Mr. Jones. Deon was supposed to be the main witness for the carjacking trial of Mr. Jones tomorrow."

"I'll check with the front desk to see if they have any information on your husband. I'll call you when I have an update."

"Thank you very much, Mr. Polansky."

Polansky quickly called Lieutenant Brianna Watkins.

"Hello, this is First Lieutenant Watkins, how can I help you?

"You'll never believe what just happened. I got a call from Deon Jenkins' wife, Ya'Lika Jenkins. She said her husband went out last night at about nine-thirty and has not returned. As you know, he is the major witness for D'Quandree Jones' carjacking trial."

"Son of a bitch. This sucks. No Jenkins. No D'Quandree Jones carjacking trial. Thanks for the heads-up detective. We'll have to get the word out and produce a major search for Jenkins."

Lieutenant Watkins ended her call with Detective Perry and dialed the telephone. "Sergeant Gillespie, this is Lieutenant Watkins. Immediately put out an all-points bulletin to locate Deon Jenkins, a key witness to the D'Quandree Jones carjacking case."

Chapter Seven

April 25, 1994, 4:35 a.m., Grim Discovery

Gerry and Vicky Birdsall walked down the stairs of the brand-new colonial they bought in Cityscape. They were excited to move to this section of Chicago and looked forward to their half-hour walk around the nearby garden-like park before they went to work.

They were unaware that on this day, their lives would be turned upside down. They loved walking through West End Park. It was close to their home, and they would have enough time to return home and get ready for work.

Not five minutes into their walk at four-thirty in the morning, Vicky noticed something covered in plastic under the branches of an old elm tree that lined the perimeter of the park. She grabbed Gerry's hand, and they slow-walked to the lump in the grass.

"What is it?" she quizzically asked her husband.

Gerry lifted a section of the dark plastic and uncovered a part of a bloody leg. "What the fuck is this?" He took out his cell phone and dialed 911 while his wife screamed in the background.

"What is your emergency?" the 911 operator asked.

"My wife and I just discovered a body covered in blood at the edge of the West End Park on Grange Street."

"Don't move. We'll have a cruiser on its way."

"I've never seen anything this gruesome in my life," stuttered Gerry to the operator and his wife. "What happened to him? Looks like he was pretty shot up."

As the words stumbled out of his mouth, they heard the blare of several police sirens and screeching brakes.

Detective Jerry Polansky, a beat officer for thirty years, approached the Birdsalls and questioned them about their early morning discovery. Polansky spoke with authority in a voice echoing his years of service as he questioned the stunned couple.

"What time did you discover the body?"

Gerry spoke first. "Four-thirty, as we began our morning walk."

"Did you see anyone leave the crime scene?" questioned Detective Joanna Sweeney, Polansky's partner.

"We looked around and didn't see anyone," added the shaking wife between sobs.

"Please stay local. We might have to have you come into the station for more questioning."

"Okay. We will be at work today if you have to talk with us."

"Okay, leave your phone numbers with that officer approaching you. Thank you for your cooperation."

"Hi, my name is Officer Longdon. May I take your phone numbers?"

"My number is 555-391-2344," stated Gerry Birdsall, "and my wife's number is 555-344-2911."

"Thank you. We will call you if we need more information," stated Officer Longdon.

Chapter Eight

April 25, 1994, 6:03 a.m., Crime Scene Unit

The crime scene soon became a jungle of Crime Scene Unit investigators. One officer roped off the area, while another officer told the crowd of onlookers to keep moving. Someone videotaped the body and the surrounding area, while another officer was sketching the whole scene. Others took pictures, while a few scoured over the victim's fingernails and accounted for each of the bullet holes.

The victim's wallet was found, and he was identified as Deon Jenkins, a twenty-nine-year-old Black male who lived at 441 Border Street, East Side Chicago.

Polansky approached Sarah Edmunds, the medical examiner, and inquired about the time of death.

Edmunds replied, "I estimate that the victim died from lead poisoning between nine p.m. and midnight last night. He's going into rigor. I'll know more once I get him on the slab."

"Thanks, Sarah."

"I am going to take another look around this area. We have to find definite proof that we can nail Jones as the killer." He continued to circle the crime scene. He bent over to pick up a matchbook from the Back Alley Bar and Restaurant. He slid it into a plastic bag. Maybe the lab could find fingerprints.

Sarah arrived at the Forensic Science Center and headed for the autopsy room. She slipped into her white coat and put on latex gloves. The body of Jenkins was already on the stainless-steel table, laying on his back with a sheet covering him.

Sarah performed autopsies at the Robert J. Stein Institute of Medicine named for Robert J. Stein, M.D. who was appointed as the first medical examiner in 1976 and served until his retirement in 1993.

Sarah was a graduate of the Boston University School of Medicine, in Massachusetts, and she experienced residency training in pathology and laboratory medicine. The department performed about seventy autopsies per year as part of its forensic pathology training.

Sarah replaced Doctor Stein after his retirement. The Medical Examiner's Office investigated any human death that dealt with criminal violence, suicide, accident, suddenly when in apparent good condition, suspicious or unusual circumstances, unlawful fetal death was provided in Public Act 100-0013 of the 101st General Assembly of Illinois.

Chapter Nine

April 25, 1994, Attorney General's Office, 9:00 a.m.

"Can someone tell me how fucking Deon Jenkins could end up dead last night?" bellowed Attorney General Alphonse Ferguson to his staff standing in the doorway of his office. "There goes my fucking carjacking case against fucking Mr. D'Quandree Jones! Fucking A, I am beyond pissed! Who was responsible for protecting Jenkins? Was it you, Callahan?"

"It was me," Gerry Fontaine, Attorney General Investigator 12, sheepishly replied. He functioned as a senior worker responsible for the most complex and sensitive Attorney General investigative assignments. "We had his apartment building covered back and front, so he must have slipped by one of our men. Maybe he went to the roof and escaped?"

"I don't care how he got away!" Ferguson yelled in Callahan's face. "The motherfucker got away, and he is dead and no good to me. The carjacking case is caput and now we have a murder case on our hands."

"Briggs, call Major Crimes and let them know that you are going to supervise this investigation," ordered Ferguson. "We have to get on top of this and find the motherfucker who snuffed Jenkins. My ass is on the chopping block with Mayor Daley, and I don't need to give him another opportunity to scrutinize our department and question our work!"

Daley had been Mayor of Chicago since 1989. He was called "the last of the big city bosses" who controlled and mobilized American cities. He was remembered for doing much to save Chicago from the declines that other rust belt cities such as Cleveland, Buffalo, and Detroit experienced during the same period.

Richard Daley played a major role in the history of the Democratic Party, especially with his support of John F. Kennedy in the presidential election of 1968. On the other hand, Daley's legacy was complicated by criticisms of his response to the Chicago riots that followed the assassination of Martin Luther King, Jr., and his handling of the notorious 1968 Democratic National Convention that happened in his city. Protest activity against the Vietnam War took place prior to and during the 1968 Democratic National Convention.

In 1968, counterculture and anti-Vietnam War protest groups began planning protests and demonstrations in response to the convention, and the city promised to maintain law and order. The protesters were met by the Chicago Police Department in the streets and parks of Chicago before and during the convention, including indiscriminate police violence against protesters, reporters, photographers, and bystanders that was later described by the National Commission on Prevention of Violence as a "police riot."

During the evening of August 28, 1968, with the police riot in full swing on Michigan Avenue in front of the Democratic party's convention headquarters, the Conrad Hilton hotel, television networks broadcast live as the anti-war protesters began the now-iconic chant "The whole world is watching".

"I'm on it," answered Larry Briggs.

Ferguson took the assignment, be it fit with his unshaken faith in the ability of the law to improve the lives of all, especially those whose economic station had forced them to live among ruthless, heavily armed gangs.

"Alphonse was very ecumenical in his work as a prosecutor," Briggs said. "It's not every day you are going to hear someone put the word prosecutor and ecumenical in the same sentence. But that's the way Alphonse approached his work... he really believed that prosecutors could do uplifting work and build communities."

"Okay, enough with the flowery descriptions. Let's get out there and find the perps who killed Jenkins."

Briggs left Ferguson's office and headed back to his unit. He waited for the elevator. The elevator doors opened, and he got in. Just as the doors were closing, a pair of hands held the doors opened and Alphonse Ferguson entered the elevator.

"Why are you still here?" bellowed the Attorney General.

"I'm on my way to the Major Crimes unit," answered Lieutenant Briggs.

"Well. All right."

Briggs left the elevator and went to his unit on the second floor. He called everyone together and ordered that Jenkins be found and found quick. "We have word, that he was found dead. We have to find out who murdered him. We have to get ahead of the fuckin' media. Get a hold of your CIs. Find out what the buzz is in the community! Any questions?"

Chapter Ten

April 25, 1994, Major Crimes Unit, 10:17 a.m.

Chicago Police Department, the Major Crimes Unit, was responsible for the investigation of all violent crimes against individuals, including homicide, sex-related crimes, robberies, and assaults. The Major Crimes Unit worked closely with victims' advocates to ensure the needs of each crime victim were met. The unit was comprised of a lieutenant, two sergeants, and fourteen detectives.

Larry Briggs arrived at the Major Crimes Unit, and he immediately went to Lieutenant Brianna Watkins's office, and closed the door.

"Hey."

She replied with "Hey," the universal greeting among law enforcement. "I bet you are here regarding the murder of Jenkins last night."

"Yep, and we'll work closely with you in his murder investigation. We blew it and couldn't keep him safe. Now we have to deal with a fuckin' murder case. Who is the lead detective on this case?"

"I am and thank you very much for giving me a high-profile murder investigation. I'm sure my staff will jump for joy with this case on top of the twelve unsolved murders that have crossed my desk in the last three months."

"We have a lot of pressure from the Mayor and Governor on this one, and I want to make sure we get the killer sooner than later."

"Okay, let's get the politics out of the way. You'll be working with Detectives Jerry Polansky and his partner Joanna Sweeney. As you know, they are our A-team, so just let them do their job."

"They have been at the crime scene since four forty-five this morning, when Jenkins' body was discovered by a couple taking their early morning walk in West End Park. We're bringing D'Quandree Jones in for questioning this morning. You might want to hang around for that interview."

"It goes without saying that Jones, that mutt, is a prime suspect in last night's murder. What was the time of death?"

Watkins replied, "The canoe maker places the time of death between nine o'clock and midnight."

"Is your A-team still at the crime scene?"

"Yeah, they are."

"Okay, I'll see what they've discovered so far. Thanks."

⁕

Briggs arrived at the crime scene and got an update from Polansky and Sweeney.

"What's up? What have you found out so far?"

"Well, we have been here since early morning and we are still scouring the crime scene for any clues to the murder of Jenkins," said Sweeney. "We are anxiously waiting for the autopsy report from Sarah Edmunds. So far, we have not found anything that can be linked to the crime."

"Okay, I'll meet you at the station later today."

Chapter Eleven

April 25, 1994, Prime Suspect Questioned, 3:30 p.m.

D'Quandree Jones was picked up at his house and brought to the sprawling police station in downtown Chicago.

Jones was brought to Sweeney's office for questioning.

Sweeney began the questioning. "Welcome, Mr. Jones. You were invited to talk with us because you are a person of interest in the murder of Jenkins last night. Please tell me where you were last night between 9:00 p.m. and midnight?"

"I'm happy to help you," replied Jones. "I was home with my old lady and homies watching TV. We were watching *Chicago Hope.*"

"Will they be able to corroborate your whereabouts last night?"

"In a heartbeat. We were drinking and eating steak."

Polansky chimed in. "Did you leave the house at all? Were you home all night?"

"Nope! Look, I told you I was home all night."

"You didn't leave the house to go to the store or to get beer?"

"Nope! Look, I told you I was home all night." Jones clenched his fists. Clearly, he wanted no part of the interview.

The questioning turned ugly as Jones became belligerent and boastful. A clenched jaw and intense eye contact manifested his anger. His fists were clenched, and his breathing became very heavy. "I don't like the idea about being dragged in for questioning about that lowlife Jenkins. I don't appreciate the fact that, again, you bastards like to try to ice me when I am innocent."

Just as his rant got louder, his attorney, Clarence Huffington, entered the room. Dressed to the nines, wearing a huge white Coleman wool felt fedora hat, deep red stunning zoot suit, Giovanni-men's-cotton-cream-ruffled-formal-dress-tuxedo, and trendy-slim-fit-shirt.

"Now, you detectives know the drill," Huffington said with a smirk. "You cannot talk with my upstanding client, Mr. Jones, without his attorney present. Mr. Jones did you say anything of consequence without my presence?"

"No, I didn't."

"If you are not going to charge my client with a crime, then we are out of here."

"It goes without saying that you are not to leave the city and be prepared to come back in for more questioning as we receive more evidence," Sweeney warned.

Sweeney and Polansky left the interrogation room and met with Lieutenant Watkins and Assistant Attorney General Briggs.

Sweeney slammed the wall with her fist in frustration. "He did it! I know he did it!"

"Well, we have to make sure that our investigation is airtight with Jones holding the gun," Polansky replied.

"You guys have to make sure we nail the son of a bitch! Without a doubt, he is the killer!" Briggs said angrily. "Bring his boys in for questioning about Jones' whereabouts last night."

Snake Eyes, Deshaun, and Washington arrived at the station and were summoned to the interrogation room. They were interviewed separately.

"Snake Eyes, you were home last night? Did D'Quandree Jones leave the house at all last night?

"No. He was home all night."

"Are you absolutely sure about that?"

"Yep. He didn't leave the house."

"Did you leave the house?"

"Nope, I was home all night."

The detectives got the same responses from Deshaun and Washington.

"Y'all may leave. Thank you for coming in on short notice."

Polansky looked at Sweeney and said it was time to go to Jenkins's house and inform his wife that they found her husband's body and that he died from gunshot wounds.

Briggs rang the doorbell and waited for the door to open. Knocking on the door, knowing he was about to destroy someone's entire world, was always the hardest thing he'd ever had to do. *No point in beating around the bush*, he thought, each time he confronted a victim's loved one.

When Ya'Lika Jenkins stood in the open door, with her three children flanking her sides, her mouth gaped open and tears welled in her eyes. She knew in her gut why law enforcement was at her door.

"Ma'am, we are sad to inform you that your husband's body was found this morning."

Ya'lika exploded with sobs and tears, as did her children. "I told him not to go. I told him that he did not have to be a hero. Oh, no! What am I going to do with my family? He had to be a hero!"

"We would like to bring you to the Medical Examiner's room to ID his body. We can wait while you get ready and get someone to watch your children. We'll be outside in the police cruiser." The detective's delivery was cold, yet routine. Being vague or indirect could've given Jenkins's wife false hope, and that would've been much worse.

Fifteen minutes later, the brand-new widow emerged from the house and joined the officers in their vehicle.

"Thank you for coming on short notice," Briggs said. "We know this is very hard for you."

Ya'lika sat in the back seat of the cruiser, peered out the window, and rode in silence, with tears streaming down her face.

Arriving at the medical examiner's office, Sarah Edmunds met Ya'Lika, Briggs, and Polansky. Victim identification was never easy for a family, and the same rang true for Edmunds. It came with the territory of the line of work she chose.

Sarah smiled at Ya'Lika. "Hello, Mrs. Jenkins."

Still looking forward, Ya'Lika's silence spoke volumes.

Sarah led the party into her office, where a picture of Deon Jenkins's body was on her desk.

Without a word, Sarah picked up the photograph and showed it to Ya'Lika Jenkins.

"Yes, this is my husband." Reduced to tears, a shocked Ya'Lika followed Sarah into a quiet room to begin her grief process.

Chapter Twelve

April 25, 1994, Triumphant Return Home, 5:00 p.m.

"I told you they had nothing on me," Jones bellowed as he entered the front door into the living room to a rousing cheer from his homies. "My carjacking case went away and, as they say, 'I got away with murder.' I'm untouchable!"

"Now let's get down to business and eat dinner. What did you cook up for dinner, bitch?" Jones asked Anodiwa.

"I didn't know what time you would be home, and I didn't prepare anything. Let's all go to Dickey's Barbecue Pit down on Essex Street. They got some mean ribs there."

"Sounds good, honey," said Jones. "I feel great, and I could eat a buffalo. Let's celebrate!"

Chapter Thirteen

April 25, 1994, Crime Scene Unit Report, 5:30 p.m.

REPORTING OFFICER NARRATIVE (Brief narrative of the facts surrounding the offense and the arrest.)

At 4:37 a.m., Dispatch received a 911 call regarding the discovery of a dead body at the West End Park at Grange Street. The caller identified himself as Gerry Birdsall (Person 1), VP Occidental Insurance. Cook County Sheriff's Unit 209 (Officer S. Mahoney) was dispatched and arrived at the scene at 4:41 a.m. After confirming the presence of the body, Reporting Officer (R/O) secured the scene and contacted Dispatch and requested backup and medical assistance. Reporting Investigators (R/Is) Detectives J. Sweeney and J. Polansky were assigned and proceeded directly to the scene. At R/Is' request, Medical Inspector S. Edmunds and a Crime Scene Unit team were notified to respond to the scene.

R/Is arrived at the scene at 6:57 a.m. and found that R/O had secured the area. Environmental conditions at the scene upon arrival are as follows: Weather: Exterior Ambient Temperature: 72° F/ 22° C; Relative Humidity: 85%; Interior Ambient

Temperature 68° F / 20° C; Interior Relative Humidity: 55%.

S. Mahoney made the following verbal report, which is stated in summary and not verbatim. R/O arrived at the scene at 4:41a.m. where R/O was met by Gerry and Vicky Birdsall (Person 2). On the side of the Park was the body of an adult male, who B. Mahoney identified as Deon Jenkins (Person 1) when he found an ID card in the victim's wallet.

After receiving the report from R/O Mahoney, R/Is conducted a preliminary inspection of the scene. On the edge of the park R/Is observed a lifeless human body, a male estimated to be in his mid 30s, lying prone on the ground. Visual inspection indicated the victim was wearing a dark jacket, white shirt and dark blue pants. The legs were slightly apart with the right leg straight and the left bent at the hip and knee. The right arm was bent slightly under the body with the hand approximately one inch from the face. The left arm was extended perpendicular to the body and bent nearly 90° at the elbow and the right was extended above the head. The head was to the north and the feet to the south. Further visual inspection revealed the back and front of the jacket and shirt were saturated with what appeared to be blood. R/Is observed multiple gunshot wounds to the face, chest, back, arms and legs. R/I delayed inspection of the body until the arrival of the Medical Examiner. CSU will conduct a thorough examination and inventory and report her findings.

Medical Examiner, Sarah Edmunds arrived at the crime scene approximately 5:21 a.m. and joined R/Is at the location of the body. Edmunds pronounced the victim deceased by visual observation that the victim was not breathing and by tactile observation that the victim did not have a palpable carotid pulse or any other indications of heartbeat or respiration. Medical Examiner Sarah Edmunds visually examined the body and observed what appeared to be multiple gunshot wounds to face, chest, stomach, arms and legs. Edmunds noted that rigor mortis was not yet evident and early indications of rigor mortis were observable on the anterior of the body and the right side of the face. She withheld an official time of death pending an autopsy report.

CSU arrived at the scene at approximately 6:03 a.m. R/Is instructed CSU to process the entire scene according to standard procedure. Preliminary search of the area for potential weapon(s) causing the injuries to the victim met with negative results. CSU will conduct a more intensive search and report their findings. R/Is left the scene at 10:00 a.m. Before leaving, R/I Sweeney instructed CSU to seal the scene at the suspension of processing. CSU to notify R/Is of progress by the end of this date. As of this filing, CSU is still actively processing at the scene.

The body of the deceased was remanded into the custody of Medical Examiner Sarah Edmunds and was removed from the scene at 7:55 a.m. The cadaver was transported to the coroner's office for autopsy. The evidence was remanded into the custody of Forensics Officer Carl Polansky for transport to the State Crime Lab for routine analysis. CSU is expected to submit an inventory of items taken into evidence within thirty days of this report, with a detailed report(s) of their findings to follow at a further date.

Polansky and Sweeney were glad to get the Crime Scene Unit report. Sweeney said, "Now we can begin the work needed to convict Jones. I cannot wait to see the smile on his face when he gets life for this murder."

Sweeney added, "We still have to wait for the ME's report and findings. That should come in a day or so once Sarah Edmunds completes her autopsy of Jenkins and reviews the lab test results."

"In the meanwhile, we can begin to pin information on our white Crime Analysis Board. We have pictures of Jenkins and Jones, photos from the murder scene, footprints, statements from the Birdsalls."

Sweeney offered the importance of this kind of detective work. "Can't tell you how many murders we have solved just taking a closer look at these boards," he said to Polansky. "Newspaper clippings, notes, maps, specific crime scene details. What one person misses, another can piece together to pin the perp."

Chapter Fourteen

April 26, 1995, 10:30 a.m.

Attorney General Ferguson was livid when he came to the office and shouted to his staff, "I just came back from court and the judge dismissed the D'Quandree Jones' carjacking trial since our eyewitness, Deon Jenkins, was murdered last night!

"Any word on the autopsy? Were we able to find any fingerprints on the expended shells or the plastic wrapping Jenkins's body? Did the autopsy reveal anything that we can use to get Jones? We must start all over again. Has anyone spoken with Sarah Edmunds? Is there an autopsy report yet? Someone go down there and find out what she has discovered!" Ferguson ordered.

"I'm on my way," answered Assistant Attorney General Larry Briggs. "I'll call you with any updates."

"That's good. We must stay ahead of this. The Governor is on my ass for results."

It was a quick ride to the Cook County morgue. Briggs greeted Sarah Edmunds.

"Good morning, Sarah."

"Good to see you, Larry. I have been working on Jenkins since seven a.m. I know this is a high-profile case and I know you need results yesterday. Jenkins was shot at close range in his head, chest, stomach, arms, and legs. He most likely died from the shot to his head and the other wounds were icing on the cake."

"I lost my carjacking case with his death. I know his demise was at the hands of D'Quandree Jones. We had him. We came very close. We'll have to go back to the drawing board and start over. Damn! I had him! I look forward to your report," said the frustrated lawmaker.

"Well, you know how thorough I am. I will notify you when I get the results."

"Okay, thanks."

"Did you know that research revealed there were 23,817 homicides in Chicago from 1965-1995," offered Briggs. "The majority of the murders took place on Saturday and Sunday."

"That is interesting," responded Sarah.

Chapter Fifteen

April 26, 1994, Noon, Seventeen Hundred Miles Away

With bags unpacked, Charlotte Steele could not wait until she was in the shower. While water splashed on her perfect body, she thought, *This shower will bring me back to Earth and I will have a wonderful time at the 53rd Los Angeles Writer's Conference. I'm so excited about being a commentator, as it enables me to meet Pulitzer Prize winner Abraham Goldstein from Israel. His documentary on Nazi German Migration to Argentina uncovered the burial plot of Adolph Hitler.*

The last few drops wiped from her curvy body, Charlotte got dressed and thought of wearing a blue, lacey Versace gown that outlined every inch of her body.

Charlotte called a cab, and the driver brought her to the front of the Beverly Hills Hilton. The Beverly Hilton appeared in giant red letters on the side of the luxurious hotel. The glamor and glitz from the people who stayed with their high-end luxury cars parked outside greeted the keynote speaker.

The driver opened the door for her. She had never seen so many limos and expensive cars in her life. The driver helped her onto the sidewalk and she thanked him with a generous tip. The glitz and ostentation of the entrance to the hotel and ballroom were impressive.

Eyes turned as she entered the luxurious International Ballroom of the Beverly Hills Hotel. The sexy investigator worked the crowd and made her way to a nice hug from Abraham Goldstein.

"It is an honor to meet you, Mr. Goldstein," the roving investigator said.

"The honor is mine to meet such a beautiful investigative reporter as you." Goldstein smiled. "I look forward to sharing the spotlight with you tomorrow on this extraordinary panel. I want to kibbutz with you later in the lounge. We have a lot to talk about."

"I would love that; I would like to hear more about your research in Argentina. I'll see you after the dinner."

Charlotte left his side and thought, *This is going to be a wonderful opportunity for me to pick his brain and gain an insight into investigative reporting at its best.*

An obnoxious banquet manager led Charlotte to the head table. Charlotte never saw anyone as full of themselves as this manager. She had a false smile and was anxious to seat Charlotte so she could get on with the preparations for the event. Charlotte thanked her, sat down, and placed her napkin on her lap.

The ballroom was well represented by national reporters from ABC, NBC, CNN, and other networks.

The speakers droned on and on throughout the affair. Charlotte immersed herself in thought of Abraham. *He is the reason why I came to this event.*

"I trust you enjoyed your meal and the speakers," the fussy manager asked, back with a very plastic smile.

"The prime rib was cooked just the way I like it and the chocolate cake drizzled with honey was decadent," Charlotte said, just before she made a mad dash for the lounge. She saw the Hitler investigator in the corner away from everyone.

"Thank you so much for meeting with me," the ancient investigator said as he kissed both sides of her cheeks and invited her to slide into the plush couch.

A cocktail waitress approached the couple and asked if they would like a drink.

"Is Amaretto okay with you?"

"Why, yes, that would be fine."

"May we have two glasses of Amaretto?"

"Okay, I'll be right back with your order," the waitress said.

"You are the only reason I came here this weekend. I have followed your marvelous work for years," Charlotte said. "You bring so much prestige to our field and I'm humbled to meet you. You show tremendous patience with your fieldwork, and it shows with your historic books, articles, and investigative reporting."

"Come, my dear, the honor is mine," Goldstein shot back. "As the arctic warms faster than any other place on the planet and sea ice declines, there is only one sure way to save polar bears from extinction and that is the reduction of human emission of greenhouse gases into the atmosphere.

"You see, I read your writing," Goldstein said with an affectionate smile. "I think it is very important that young investigative reporters bring so much meaning to the future of this planet. I am ancient, and it is time we pass the baton to you and other bright reporters around the world. I spent five years talking with Argentine leaders, rabbis, Jewish congregants, Catholic priests, and hundreds of Argentine citizens. It was a lot of work, and I am tired. I cannot do this any longer."

"OY, mein back and legs. Too much pain." Goldstein moaned. "Up and down the stairs, these Argentine buildings do not have elevators. I had to investigate where the hunches brought me, and I'm finished."

Goldstein continued before Charlotte had a chance to say anything. "I am going to retire and spend what time I have left with my family. You are young, and you have many years left in the tank. I tell you what I am going to do. As I hear of issues that need reporting, I will call you and give you the heads up. I know that you can carry my torch and give the world the information it needs to prevent killing and ending life on earth as we know it."

The waitress returned with their glasses of Amaretto.

Goldstein shared some facts about the Amaretto with Charlotte. "Amaretto has been around for centuries. The Italian, almond-flavored digestif is one of several sweet liqueurs that experienced its heyday in America during the mid-twentieth century. It tastes like almonds, but most amaretto actually gets its flavor from apricot kernels, or pits.

"Disaronno, the amaretto brand with which you're most likely familiar, claims to use the very first amaretto recipe, which dates back to 1525. Aside from apricot kernels and sugar, though, the recipe is a secret."

Charlotte smiled. "Well, aren't you the world expert on liqueurs?"

"The real origin of Amaretto may be lost to history, but the legend of its creation is alive and well and dates back almost five hundred years. In the town of Serono in northwest Italy, Leonardo da Vinci's assistant, Bernardino Luini, was commissioned to do a fresco of the Virgin Mary inside a church. He chose a local woman to be his model, and she was so honored she wanted to give Luina a gift. She couldn't afford to buy him something expensive, so she steeped apricot kernels in brandy and the first bottle of Amaretto was born."

"Well, that is fascinating. I'm impressed with your vast grasp of knowledge. So, tell me more about your research in South America regarding the migration of Nazis to Argentina. Many say Hitler was buried in Germany, but you found evidence of his demise in Argentina. What were your findings about Adolph Hitler and where he is buried?"

"Well, there is still a lot of research being done on this subject. We know Adolf Eichman was found in San Fernando, Buenos Aires by the Mosad. He made his way to Argentina by the 'rat route,' which provided a safe haven for thousands of Nazi criminals.

"Eichmann was brought to Israel and was tried and found guilty as one of the architects of the 'Final Solution' of Europe's Jews. We don't know what happened to Adolph Hitler's body since there are many rumored stories that he was brought to Argentina. More research needs to be done on this subject."

"Well, I am humbled by your confidence in me. It is a wonderful offer. I don't know what to say. I am honored by your request. Maybe I will find the remains of Adolph Hitler."

"Well, you will do it?" Goldstein asked.

"Yes, I will. I am in shock. This is so overwhelming that you have that much trust in me to deliver?"

"Enough said. Let's shake on it." Goldstein extended his wrinkled hand.

She shook his hand. "I accept."

"Let's raise a toast to our agreement." Goldstein offered.

They ended their conversation and exited to their rooms.

During the panel discussion the following day, she reflected on her momentous weekend. She was overwhelmed at the reception of her presentation and was pleased at the questions she had to handle following her presentation.

Chapter Sixteen

July 1, 1994, Noon—"There is hope"

Larry Briggs would not let the carjacking case or Jenkins's murder go unsolved. He pored over the evidence several times and he could see a way to charge D'Quandree Jones with the carjacking and murder.

Briggs discussed the case with Joanna Sweeney, "We thought we had Jones in the carjacking case when we had Deon Jenkins as an eyewitness. Now with Jenkins dead, we must start over."

"We talked with Jones and his boys to try to pin Jones with Jenkins's murder, but we hit a brick wall," added Sweeney. "Unfortunately, we put all our eggs in one basket with Jenkins as our star witness, and we didn't focus on any other evidence that would allow us to put Jones away on the carjacking, never mind the murder of Jenkins."

"Maybe, we can convict Jones on the carjacking and we would be able to put Jones away for some time. You know, like what happened to Al Capone. The government could not convict him on any of the murders that he committed or his drugs or sex trafficking. However, they were able to find him guilty on tax evasion and we were able to put his ass in jail. Maybe we can have the same luck with Jones. Let's take another look at the evidence in the carjacking case."

Briggs noted that the carjacking took place on Orchard Street in front of a row of stores. He couldn't find any videos from their security systems, so he and Sweeney would pay a visit to each of the stores on Orchard Street to track down any available videos for the night of the murder of Jenkins.

Their first stop was Gloria's Variety, and they went through the front door and asked to speak with the owner. A short Italian lady came forward. "I'm the owner. My name is Gloria Muzzi. How can I help you?"

The smell of fresh vegetables and fruits flowed from inside the store.

"My name is Larry Briggs, Deputy Attorney General for the state of Illinois and this is Detective Joanna Sweeney from the Chicago Police Department. We are investigating a carjacking that took place on your block and we are wondering if you have any video from the morning of April 24, 1993."

"I'm sorry. I cannot help you. My system has been down for the past three years, and I didn't find it necessary to restore it."

"Okay, thanks anyway, but you probably should look into restoring your surveillance system. You don't know, someday you may need it. Have a good day."

Briggs and Sweeney entered the second store, Ed's Complete Computer Works. "I'd like to speak with the owner."

"My name is Ed Kelley. How can I help you?

"My name is Larry Briggs, Deputy Attorney General for the state of Illinois and this is Detective Joanna Sweeney from the Chicago Police Department. We are investigating a carjacking that took place on your block and we are wondering if you have any video from the morning of April 24, 1993."

"Well, I do have a security system and I've had it since January 1, 1992. I don't save the tapes, but you can contact Blackwater Security First, and they may have it. They monitor my system, and they may have what you are looking for. They are located at 1401 First Street, here in Chicago."

"Thanks. You have been very helpful."

Briggs entered the next store, Acer Hardware. "I'd like to speak with the owner."

"The owner is not here right now, but you can speak with me. My name is Frank Darcey, General Manager."

"My name is Larry Briggs, Deputy Attorney General for the state of Illinois and this is Detective Joanna Sweeney from the Chicago Police Department. We are investigating a carjacking that took place on your block and we are wondering if you have any video from the morning of April 24, 1993."

"We do have a security system, but we only keep tapes for six months and then we reuse them. Sorry I cannot help you."

"That's okay. Thanks. Have a good day."

Briggs thought he would cut his losses, and they went to Blackwater Security First to see if he would have any luck finding what he needed.

It took them twenty minutes to reach the company, and he buzzed them into the lobby. He asked the receptionist to talk with the owner. He was told to sit and wait, and he would be paged.

After ten minutes, a well-dressed woman who identified herself as Alice McCormick, the owner, greeted him. "Follow me to the conference room."

Once inside the conference room, Briggs introduced himself. "Hi, my name is Larry Briggs, Deputy Attorney General for the state of Illinois and this is Detective Joanna Sweeney from the Chicago Police Department. We are investigating a carjacking that took place on your block and we are wondering if you have any video from the morning of April 24, 1993."

"We are investigating a carjacking that took place on the block of 1551 Locke Street. You monitor a video system for Acer Hardware, and they referred us to you. I am wondering if you have any video from the morning of April 24, 1993."

"Well, that is a while ago. Let me call my system manager." Picking up the phone, she placed the call. "Hello, John, this is Alice. Do we happen to have videotapes from Acer Hardware on April 24, 1993?"

"Let me check and I'll call you right back."

"That's good. I'm in the first-floor conference room."

"Give me five minutes."

"Okay."

Hanging up the phone, Alice looked at Briggs. "I hope we can help you. John will call me right back."

Within minutes, the phone rang.

"Hi John, you found something? I'll be right up." Nodding, Alice hung up the phone. "Follow me, Mr. Briggs and Ms. Sweeney."

Briggs, Sweeney and Alice got off the elevator on the third floor and she asked them to follow her into the technical division of the company.

"Hi, John. This is Mr. Briggs and Detective Sweeney, and they are investigating a carjacking that took place in front of Acer Hardware. You said you had some tapes."

John nodded and motioned toward the three chairs. "Please, have a seat in front of the video screen and we will review the tapes. The tape you are looking for began at midnight. Let's watch it and tell me when you want me to stop it."

The tape played until five o'clock in the morning when Briggs asked John to stop the tape and back it up slowly. He did and played it forward and there it was: a Black man breaking into a baby blue 1992 Cadillac Coupe DeVille. He jumped the wires and drove off.

"That's it. May I have a copy of that tape?"

"No problem. It will take an hour to copy it and we'll bring it to your office when the job is complete."

"Well, thank you very much, Ms. McCormick. You just made our day."

"That's great. Nice meeting you and I'll talk with you later."

Briggs and Sweeney returned to the police headquarters with broad smiles as they made their way to Lieutenant Watkins's office. "You will never guess what we saw today!"

"Okay what?"

"We just returned from Blackwater Security First. They will deliver a copy of a tape we watched that showed a Black man stealing the car involved in the carjacking case of D'Quandree Jones. I don't know if it showed Jones stealing the car, but we will know in a short while."

"Well, that is great. Maybe this case isn't dead after all."

"We'll have to wait and see."

"Lieutenant Briggs, there is a package for you from a security company. Come get it," said the desk sergeant of the day.

"I'll be right down."

Briggs retrieved the package and headed for the office of the media specialist. He dug out the CD from the box and put it into the TV and started playing it. The CD showed an African American male entering a Cadillac, jumping the wires, and driving off.

"Please rewind the CD from the point the African American approached the vehicle."

The media specialist did as requested.

"Please highlight the African American male and focus on his face," Briggs said. "Can you zero in on his face?

"How is this?" asked the police media specialist.

"That's it. Yes, that is Jones. We got him. Did we get any fingerprints from the Cadillac? Any DNA?

"I don't know. I'll check the file."

"Call me when you get the results."

"Okay."

Briggs returned to his office and waited for the update. He thought, *We got him. We got him this time.* His phone rang.

"Hello, this is Larry Briggs, Deputy Attorney General. May I help you.?"

"Mr. Briggs, this is Frank Darcey from police headquarters. I completed my search from the carjacking file, and I found fingerprint and DNA evidence. We compared these results with D'Quandree Jones, and we found a DNA match with Jones."

"Thank you very much, Frank. Please expedite those results to my office. I'll be in touch if I need further assistance."

"Okay. Send me what you have."

Briggs brought these recent developments to Alphonse Ferguson, Attorney General. "Sir, your carjacking case is not dead. We had Deon Jenkins as a witness and did not go deeper into the case because we had Jenkins. Since Jenkins is dead, I went back into the case file and discovered there is a videotape of the perp stealing the Cadillac. It is D'Quandree Jones. We also found DNA that matches Jones and fingerprints matching Jones."

"Shit, that is great. Make sure you bring all these new developments once you receive them. Good news. We'll get that bastard, Jones."

"Yes, we will."

Chapter Seventeen

July 5, 1994, 9:00 a.m.

Attorney General Ferguson met with his staff to go over the evidence for the D'Quandree Jones carjacking case.

"Okay, Briggs, tell me how we are going to win this case."

"Good morning, General. As requested, here are the video, fingerprints, and DNA information on the stolen Cadillac," said Briggs. "Our experts have confirmed these results. They will stand up in court."

"Good work, Briggs. You better be right. We can't lose this one again. We must put Jones behind bars. He has been running free too long. He is a menace to our community, and we must stop his drugs and sex traffic. I can now reopen the carjacking case and we'll get that motherfucker, D'Quandree Jones. I will file for a new trial today and we'll begin the process all over again."

Attorney General Ferguson immediately headed for the Clerk of Courts and filed a new motion to retry D'Quandree Jones with carjacking.

Chapter Eighteen

July 5, 1994, 10:00 p.m.

"Hey guys, let's head over to Washington Avenue," said D'Quandree Jones. "I hear there is a big delivery of coke going down. We need to cop that shipment and make a few million ourselves."

Jones and his gang jumped into three vehicles and sped off for Washington Avenue. They arrived at 49 Washington Avenue and stormed the building with the sound of automatic weapon fire breaking the silence of the night. They were able to shoot their way to the third-floor apartment where the crack was stored.

Jones yelled, "Break down the fuckin' door!" He entered the apartment with guns blazing and they were able to reach the stash with no more opposition. They packed the bricks into bags and carried them. "This is quite a haul," Jones yelled with a "whoop, whoop."

They rushed down the stairs over fallen bodies and quickly made their escape back to the gang lair.

"We must have ten bricks of this shit or maybe more," said Jones. "Let's divide it up. We'll keep some for ourselves and the rest we will sell on the street."

Jones broke off a bit of the coke and put it in a pipe and smoked it. He sat back in his recliner and felt a rush that made him close his eyes and shiver with pleasure. He backed up his smoke with a beer. "Now, that is what I'm talking about. This shit is good. We'll make a few bucks with this fuckin' shit. Yeah, baby!"

"Hey, boss, we hit the mother lode!" Snake Eyes yelled.

Chapter Nineteen

July 7, 1994, 9:30 a.m.

Lieutenant Briggs and two other officers left police headquarters and headed to D'Quandree Jones' house to pick him up and bring him in for questioning. They arrived at the house and rang the doorbell. The door opened.

A gang member stood in the door. "Can I help you?"

"Yeah, we are looking for D'Quandree Jones. Is he home?

"Wait one minute. Ree! The gendarmes are here."

D'Quandree came to the door with a smile. "Well, hello gentlemen. What can I do for you this glorious morning?"

"We are here to take you to police headquarters. We have probable cause that you were involved in a carjacking. We are here to arrest you and bring you to police headquarters," said Briggs as he handcuffed Jones and walked him toward the cruiser. "You have the right to remain silent and refuse to answer questions. Anything you say can and will be used against you in a court of law. You have the right to speak to an attorney before speaking to the police and to have an attorney present during the questioning now or in the future. If you cannot afford an attorney, one will be appointed for you before any questioning. If you decide to answer questions now without an attorney present, you will still have the right to stop answering at any time until you talk to an attorney. Knowing and understanding your rights as I have explained them to you, are you willing to answer my questions without an attorney present?"

"Well, what the fuck is this about?"

"Lower your head and get into the cruiser. We'll talk once we get to headquarters."

"Okay, do what the fuck you have to do."

Once at the headquarters, Jones was booked, and his charges were recorded. He had several mug shots. All his personal items were removed, to be returned upon release. And his fingerprints were taken. He submitted to a body search as he was frisked, and a search was made to locate any outstanding warrants. He was also screened for contagious diseases such as tuberculosis, HIV positive or AIDS. He was then brought to the interrogation room.

"As I said when we picked you up, we have probable cause that you were involved in a carjacking. This is a Class 1 Felony theft, and it generally carries a sentence of imprisonment ranging from four to 15 years in prison time and a fine up to $25,000, plus payment of restitution for losses associated with the theft of a vehicle valued between $10,000 and $100,000."

"Wait a fuckin' minute. You already tried that, and the case was dismissed. I have double jeopardy here. You cannot hold me. You tried and you lost."

Briggs answered, "We have an arrest warrant that states that you hijacked a car, and we have video, fingerprint and DNA evidence that you committed that crime."

"That's bullshit. Let me get the fuck out of here."

Jones didn't have to wait long when he heard, "Come on, let's go. It's time to go before the judge who will determine your bail."

Jones was brought to court for his bail hearing. There were people running around and providing information to the bailiff. Arrested individuals were trying to find out what was happening with their lawyers. Bail was set for others. There was bail negation. There was total confusion but, somehow it all made sense.

It was Jones' chance to appear before the judge to discuss his bail.

Judge Carlos Sanchez advised Jones of his constitutional rights. "You are charged with Theft by Unauthorized Control of Property exceeding $10,000 and not exceeding $100,000. You intended to deprive the owner permanently of the use of the property. Here is a copy of the charges."

"How do you plead? Guilty or not guilty?"

"Not guilty."

"I set your bail at $150,000."

"I'll call my boys and I will post bail myself."

"Okay," said the judge.

Jones was brought back to the holding cell waiting for him to post bail. Jones looked around the cell and there were all kinds of men waiting for their arraignments. There were domestic abusers, gangbangers, murderers, purse snatchers. Some were covered in tattoos while others just had an onery look about them. This would be a perfect crew for a pirate ship.

Snake Eyes Washington arrived at the court and posted Jones' $15,000 bail.

Jones returned to the court to wait for Judge Sanchez.

Judge Sanchez acknowledged receipt of the bail and stated a Preliminary Hearing was scheduled for November 7, 1994 at 9:00 a.m.

"Thanks for coming, man. Let's get the fuck out of here. This place fuckin' freaks me out."

Chapter Twenty

July 5, 1994, 10:00 p.m.

Feeling frustrated and with no hope for the future, Jones rallied his boys, and they left the house looking to "beat niggas" and score some bricks. They headed to Koreatown where there was a one-in-twenty chance of being a crime victim for each year spent within the neighborhood limits.

By the 1980s and 1990s, the neighborhood fell into a deeper slum and now Four Corner Hustlers were selling drugs in even higher quantity than the Souls and Vice Lords. Gang wars ripped through the neighborhood and a legendary drug ring continued to successfully operate in the neighborhood.

Gangs, drugs, and violence were still issues in this community, and this neighborhood was considered a very dangerous neighborhood. West Garfield Park had been credited with having one of the most sophisticated drug rings in Chicago.

This area was severely blighted with several shuttered homes and businesses, many of which had been vacant for many decades. Many deteriorated buildings had been torn down over the years, leaving several vacant lots. The population had also been sharply dropping since the 1970s when the population was over 48,000. Now the population is around 18,000 and dropping. West Garfield Park struggled with high rates of poverty and severe disinvestment and was one of the more deteriorated communities of Chicago.

D'Quandree got home and called his attorney, Clarence Huffington. "Hey, man! What the fuck is up? I just spent a day in court on charges stemming from that carjacking thing. I thought that case was gone. What about double jeopardy?"

"Stay cool, man! Come into my office tomorrow morning at nine and we'll talk. In the meantime, I'll call the court and see what's up. See you tomorrow."

Jones hung up the phone and yelled, "What the fuck? Can't I get a motherfucking break?"

"It's okay, honey, here is a beer and just sit and chill," said Anodiwa. "Ain't nothing you can do about it until you talk with your attorney tomorrow."

"Fuck. Where's my white lady? I need to mellow."

"Here it is, boss."

"Now you are talking. Get me my pipe." Jones filled his pipe and smoked until he fell back in his chair, and he was a mellow fellow. "That's what I'm talking about. They ain't going to get me in white man's cages. I'm going to beat this rap." Jones drifted off to sleep for the night.

The next morning, Jones was at Clarence Huffington's office precisely at nine o'clock. "Okay. I'm here. What is going to happen to my $15,000?"

"Have a seat, D'Quandree. I called the court yesterday and they told me they have new evidence in the carjacking scheme, and they plan to try to convict you for that crime."

"I thought it was gone once Jenkins was dead and they no longer had an eyewitness."

"Well, they came up with new evidence. They have a videotape of you stealing the car. They also have fingerprint and DNA evidence. I guess they thought once they had an eyewitness, they didn't have to dig any further.

"Looks like they may have something on you. I looked at what they have. But we'll tear it apart and try to find daylight to set you free," Clarence Huffington offered. "Their shit looks good. They got you on tape. They have your fingerprints in the Cadillac and have matched your DNA on the steering wheel.

"You gotta be shittin' me. I have to go before the judge again?"

"We will obviously challenge their results. My team will begin to develop our defense. We will meet again in a few weeks."

Chapter Twenty-One

October 12, 1994

Charlotte Steele finished her writing for the day and went to The Italian Village owned by the Capitanini family since 1927. This downtown Italian Village was Chicago's oldest Italian restaurant. During its 90 years in business, Italian Village had dished out nine million meals and employed more than 40,000 Chicagoans. Four current employees had been with the restaurant for over fifty years.

Charlotte walked up to the hostess and was greeted by a sign that read: Buonappetito (good appetite or enjoy your meal). Behind the hostess were pictures on the wall of celebrities who ate at the restaurant over the years and, of course, the counter displayed hats, cups, t-shirts and other drink containers decorated with Italian pictures.

Charlotte was always amused at the sky-blue ceilings dotted with stars in the brightly colored bar area complete with Roman statues and columns. Charlotte was brought to a private area which gave you an intimate feeling of dining.

A waiter introduced himself as Antonio and asked if she cared for a cocktail.

"Thank you. I'd like to order Alfred's Sazerac Bulleit Rye with Orange Bitters and Angave Nectar stirred and served neatly in a Pernod rinsed glass."

"Would you care for an appetizer?"

"No, thank you."

"Very well, I will bring your drink."

Charlotte perused the dinner menu and settled for Lobster Fettucine Alfredo with tender ribbons of pasta tossed with Maine lobster meat, diced tomato, mushrooms and green onions in Alfredo sauce. She placed her order when Antonio returned with her drink.

The relaxed investigator sipped her drink and looked around the dining room. She could see that the restaurant was as busy as it usually was at dinnertime. She dug into her briefcase and took out her latest work, *The Genocide of 800,000 Tutsi, as well as Twa and moderate Hutu.* The massacre was carried out between April 7, 1994 and July 15, 1994, during the Rwandan Civil War.

She was writing an in-depth account of the genocide for *The New York Times.* The scale and brutality of the massacre shocked worldwide, but no country intervened to forcefully stop the killings. The militia murdered victims with machetes and rifles. An estimated 250,000 to 500,000 women were raped during The Genocide.

Charlotte's sources told her that the killing hadn't stopped, but it was very difficult to get information at all.

Charlotte's dinner arrived, and she put her research aside. She savored every morsel and thoroughly enjoyed her meal.

She waved down the waiter. "Antonio, everything was wonderful. May I have my check?"

"I'll be right back." He cleared the table.

Charlotte paid her bill and left the restaurant, and headed home. She had had a long day, and she wanted to hug her pillow.

Chapter Twenty-Two

November 7, 1994

"All rise. This court with the Honorable Judge Marsha A. Fielding presiding is now in session. Please be seated and come to order," bellowed the Bailiff.

Judge Fielding reported, "I will decide whether sufficient evidence exists to send your case to the Superior Court for trial. Today will determine whether there is probable cause to believe a crime was committed and whether there is probable cause to believe the person in front of the court is the one who committed the crime. Is the prosecution prepared to begin?"

"Yes, Your Honor," replied Ralph Emerson, the prosecutor.

"Is the defense prepared for the hearing?"

"We are, Your Honor," said Clarence Huffington.

"Mr. Emerson, you may proceed."

"Thank you, Your Honor. I would like to ask the court to accept an eyewitness account offered by Deon Jenkins, who was murdered during the first trial against Mr. D'Quandree Jones based on Rule 804. Here is a copy of Mr. Jenkins' death certificate. We ask that his deposed statement that he saw D'Quandree Jones steal the Cadillac from the prior trial against Mr. Jones be used for this trial.

"We also want to enter into evidence the video of Mr. Jones stealing the Cadillac in this carjacking case, and we will present Alice McCormick, owner of Blackwater Security First, as a witness."

"Mr. Huffington, do you have anything you want to add at this hearing?"

"Your Honor, thank you. First of all, we object to the use of Rule 804 regarding Mr. Jenkins's prior deposition. While we were present at his deposition, we were unable to depose him because he was murdered the day after the deposition began."

"As for the video of Mr. Jones allegedly stealing a car, we are ready to prove that he was not the individual in that video. Furthermore, we object that the fingerprints found in the stolen car belonged to Mr. Jones at the time of the carjacking."

"Thank you very much, gentlemen. I will take the testimony given today and render my decision tomorrow at nine a.m. If there is nothing more, court is adjourned."

Clarence Huffington left the hearing and returned to his office. He called D'Quandree Jones. "D'Quandree, I just left a preliminary hearing for you. The prosecution said they have a video of a black man stealing the Cadillac and they want to present Rule 804, which will allow them to use Deon

Jenkins' deposition for your last case. We have to return to court tomorrow to hear whether the judge will find there is probable cause to continue the case against you."

"When is this shit going to end? I should have double jeopardy and be done with it."

"Well, I explained to you before that they have new evidence, and they have the right to pursue another trial. Just relax, we will hear the judge's decision tomorrow."

"Fuck it. Call me tomorrow."

Chapter Twenty-Three

November 8, 1994

Clarence Huffington packed his briefcase and arrived on time for court with D'Quandree Jones.

"All rise. This court with the Honorable Judge Marsha A. Fielding presiding is now in session. Please be seated and let the court come to order."

"Today, I have determined there is probable cause that a crime was committed. There is probable cause to believe the person in front of the court is the one to commit the crime.

"I have decided that sufficient evidence exists to send your case, D'Quandree Jones, to the Superior Court for trial. The court date will be set by the Superior Court, and they will notify you when the case will be heard. Court is adjourned."

Mr. Huffington and Jones left the courtroom and sat on a bench outside the court.

"What now, Mr. Lawyer?"

"Well, the judge found probable cause and they will take the case to Superior Court and try you for carjacking. As you know, my team and I will continue to work on your defense, and I feel things are moving in the right direction."

"Yeah. What fucking direction is that? I am not going to jail. I am not going to fucking jail!"

"Let's get together next week and we will see what evidence the prosecution is presenting to the court."

"Okay, but I'm telling you again. I am not going to jail. No how!"

The sky was cloudy, and it was seasonably warm at sixty degrees as Jones left the courthouse. He was wearing jeans with a blue shirt and a plaid sport coat as he made his way to his car. It was a short ride home, and he arrived at home with everyone talking at once.

"How did it go?"

"Just hold on, you punk-ass bitches. It ain't over yet. The motherfucking Attorney General Ferguson ain't done with me yet. The judge said I have to go on trial for the carjacking."

"What did you say?" asked Snake Eyes. "I thought you got off with double fucking jeopardy."

"Nope. They want another piece of me."

"Well, what are you going to do?"

"I gotta wait and see what my lawyer can do for me. He said my case looks good. At least, that is what he said."

Chapter Twenty-Four

November 14, 1994

Jones arrived at his lawyer's office promptly at 9:30 a.m.

"Well, have you figured out how I'm staying out of jail?"

"Not quite yet. We are still working on that. Your trial is set for August 12, 1995. We'll be ready for your case by then. We will rebut their findings by then."

"When will we be able to review the new evidence that the prosecution has?"

"I've requested a copy of all of their evidence, and as soon as I receive it, I will call you to come to the office and we will review it together."

"I think this is bullshit. They already dismissed the case once and now they want to open things up again. This is crazy."

"Chill. We will see what they have. Go home and I will notify you when to come back to the office."

"Okay."

D'Quandree was steaming on his way to his car. He was just getting used to feeling free and now this. He opened the window in his car and looked out to the buildings as he drove home. *No way am I going to prison. This shit has to stop. He yelled, "Fuck!"*

He arrived home and his boys began questioning him as he walked through the door.

"What up boss?" asked Snake Eyes

"Yeah, what's going on? Echoed the rest of the boys.

"My lawyer said they have new evidence to prove I murdered fuckin Deon Jenkins. Supposedly they have a video of the car being hijacked and they have fingerprints. My lawyer is going to call me in once he gets the new shit from the prosecution."

"That's bullshit," said Snake Eyes. "Why don't they leave you alone?"

"You got that right."

Chapter Twenty-Five

November 28, 1994—"Wrong Person"

The phone was ringing and D'Quandree picked up the phone, "Who is this"

"D'Quandree, please come to the office. This is Clarence Huffington. I received the information that we were looking to review from the prosecution."

"Okay, I'll be right there."

D'Quandree jumped in his car and sped to the lawyer's office.

D'Quandree arrived at the office and was brought into the conference room.

"Good, you are here. I received the evidence that the prosecution has for their case against you.

First of all, they are using the deposition of Deon Jenkins while he was still alive. They want to use an eyewitness account offered by Deon Jenkins, who was murdered during the first trial against Mr. D'Quandree Jones based on Rule 804. Here is a copy of Mr. Jenkins's death certificate. We ask that his deposed statement that he saw D'Quandree Jones steal the Cadillac from the prior trial against Mr. Jones be used for this trial.

"I objected to the admission of his deposition and the judge is going to rule on this request. He was allegedly murdered the day after the deposition began and we did not have an opportunity to depose Jenkins before his death."

"They also entered the video of Mr. Jones stealing the Cadillac in this carjacking case, and they presented Alice McCormick, owner of Blackwater Security First as a witness."

"As for the video of Mr. Jones allegedly stealing a car, we are ready to prove that he was not the individual in that video. Furthermore, we object that the fingerprints found in the stolen car belonged to Mr. Jones at the time of the carjacking."

When is this shit going to end? I should have double jeopardy and be done with it.

Chapter Twenty-Six

July 10, 1995

About two weeks before the scheduled trial for the murder of Jenkins, D'Quandree Jones pulled Snake Eyes Washington outside on the porch and told him he was concerned about the upcoming trial.

"Never mind, I have an idea," said Jones.

The next day, D'Quandree took Snake Eyes across the street from the District Court House and waited for Attorney General Alphonse Ferguson to come out of the courthouse.

Jones gave Snake Eyes a notebook and some cash for the train and asked him to follow Ferguson home. "Write down where he goes. Does he talk with anyone, and where does he get off?"

Ferguson got off the train at Clinton Station, and Snake Eyes followed him to his car.

"I'm done following him and now I can go home and report all of this to D'Quandree."

Snake Eyes met Jones at his house later that night.

"Well, what you got?" Jones asked.

"I did what you told me. I followed Ferguson to Clinton Station where he got off and I followed him to his car. I wrote down his plate number and the make of Ferguson's car. He didn't talk with anyone on the ride to his car."

"Good work."

Chapter Twenty-Seven

July 12, 1995, Killer Heatwave, 9:30 a.m.

Charlotte Steele walked into the *Chicago Tribune*, formerly known as the "Greatest Newspaper in the World," sweating profusely because of the intense heat wave that hit the Chicago area and the rest of the Midwest.

She went directly to the Investigative News Department, headed by Chief Editor, Tom Falcone. Tom was a tall, obese man wearing black pants, a white shirt with plaid suspenders, and a wrinkled face. He had a big red nose and white hair because of thirty-five years at the paper and visiting local pubs after work.

She greeted him with a strong, wet handshake. "Hey, Tom. Pretty fucking hot, huh?"

Falcone replied, "You isn't shitting. This heat wave has already killed 239 elderly. The elderly are afraid to open their windows or go outside for fear of crime. I hope we are coming to the end of the vicious crime death rate in this city. That is, I hope the trend is moving down. I want you to find out what's up with this intense heat and how long do we have to put up with it," bellowed the editor, counting the days to his retirement.

"I'm on it, Tom." Steele nodded. "I also heard that there are deaths in St. Louis and Milwaukee."

"We don't have a lot of time, so get on it."

Public officials shrugged off the high temperatures, thinking that this was just another summer scorcher. However, they quickly changed their minds as bodies began arriving at the Cook County Medical Examiner's office on Chicago's west side. Dozens came at once. So many came that the morgue commandeered refrigerated trucks to handle the overflow.

In just a few days, the extreme summer heat killed 739 Chicagoans.

"I have a friend who works at the National Weather Service in Roansville, Illinois. It is one of only two National Weather Service stations in Illinois," replied Steele. "I'll give her a call and see what they have." Steele turned to leave.

Charlotte walked to her car, wiping her forehead on the way as the heat hit her like a category 2 hurricane. Once inside her car, she called the Roansville weather facility as she plugged in the numbers and heard the phone ringing. She was anxious to talk with Heather Frost, Chief Meteorologist of Roansville National Weather Service.

"National Weather Service. This is Heather Frost. May I help you?"

"Heather, how have you been? This is Charlotte Steele."

"Hi, Charlotte, good to hear from you! I don't know what is going on with this heat!"

"And that is exactly what I wanted to discuss with you. This "heat wave" is wreaking havoc with everyone; it came out of nowhere and I'm trying to find out if there is any relief in sight. I thought if anyone knows the answer to these questions, it's gotta be you."

"Well, we have been tracking this weather system as it traveled from the west coast," replied Heather. The heat wave was led by a large high-pressure system that traversed across the Midwest United States. This system was consistently producing maximum temperatures in the nineties during the day, with minimum temperatures still remaining as high as the eighties at night, which is abnormal for Midwest summer months. The system also brought extremely low wind speeds, along with the high humidity."

"When is it likely to leave us?" asked Charlotte.

"The poorest citizens are paying for this intense heat, and we haven't provided the resources to deal with an event of nature like this. I learned at the last City Council meeting that public officials have announced free water and fans are available at most churches, fire, and police stations. Also, there are a few mobile units circulating through the city offering first aid treatment. Now you are up-to-date," offered the beleaguered weather person.

"What are the projections for when the heat wave will leave us?"

"A 'stuck' high-pressure system can keep a large mass of hot, dry air parked over the region for weeks. The latest satellite projections have this system moving east in a day or so," replied Heather. "The system will leave us, but we will still be plagued by the heat for another week or so. This system is a one-hundred-year phenomenon."

"Well, thank you so much for the update, and it is good to see what the city is doing with free water and fans. I must run. More phone calls. Take care, Heather."

"Good to hear from you. We'll have to do dinner sometime."

"Good idea. Let's hope the weather clears fast so we can do that."

Charlotte went home to get out of the killer heat. She wiped the sweat from her dripping forehead and sat down at the computer with a glass of iced water to do her own research. She took a shower and got in clean clothes before she worked on the article. Charlotte worked into the night and finished her project.

Chapter Twenty-Eight

July 12, 1994, D-Day

Attorney General Alphonse Ferguson wrapped up his four o'clock staff meeting.

"Thank you all so much for all the time and effort you put into the D'Quandree Jones case. We will begin the process tomorrow to put him away for life. Have a great evening and see you in court tomorrow. Good night, all."

"Good night to you, sir," responded Deputy Attorney General Susan Weaver.

Ferguson went back to his office, put the court papers in his briefcase, and looked at his family pictures on his desk. He was proud of his wife, who helped to raise their three boys. He locked his door and made his way to Clark/Lake Station, a short distance from the courthouse.

The crusader Attorney General bought a coffee and a copy of the *Chicago Sun-Times*. He arrived at the Blue Line track and waited for his ride to Clinton Station.

The train came, and he began his journey. He got his seat by the window and sat down to read his paper and drink his coffee. He occasionally looked out the window as the train made its way through working neighborhoods in Chicago.

Ferguson reflected on his day. He thought, *After dinner tonight, I must put the finishing touches on my opening statement. I need to make sure my case is airtight against D'Quandree Jones. I cannot let him walk with the murder of Deon Jenkins, a major witness in Jones's carjacking case. The carjacking charges stemmed from an incident that occurred in June 1994, between Jones and Deshaun Jackson.*

A tired Ferguson closed his eyes as his thoughts were focused on his team meeting today and he thought about his devoted collection of prosecutors who were determined to win this case.

Ferguson looked out the window and took his last sip of coffee, thinking, *The men and women who prosecute criminals are those who seek justice and dedicate their careers to convicting the guilty and keeping society safe. Their jobs, however, can carry serious risks. They are the people criminals often blame for their convictions, and a grudge can have dangerous consequences. For some individuals, they feel actions are needed to exact revenge on those perceived to have wronged them and, in their eyes, prevented them from living their lives.*

D'Quandree Jones was brought before Judge Mary Simpson many times before, and she had been unable to convict him in all of his trials. Jones felt his luck was running out and a strong case was mounting against him in the murder of Deon Jenkins.

Chapter Twenty-Nine

July 12, 1995, 4:30 p.m.

D'Quandree Jones jumped out of the car driven by Snake Eyes and told him to meet him at the rendezvous point.

Jones slowly walked toward the back of the Clinton Station parking lot and hid in the bushes. Sweat was pouring down his forehead from the killer heat wave that plagued the Chicago area.

Ferguson had been on D'Quandree's mind all night to the point of him losing sleep. He knew Ferguson wanted to ruin his life. He'd worked hard to build up his reputation and he wasn't going to allow some whitey to blow it for him.

"Ferguson, the Jeb End, is going down," D'Quandree mumbled under his breath.

Since he was early, he would use that time to plan how he was going to waste him. *I'm going to walk to his car and just as he slides into the front seat, I'm going to yell, "Hey, ratfucker, freeze!" I want him to see who is going to get him to ride the pale horse.* D'Quandree smiled wickedly at his thoughts. Nodding, he thought, *I'm going to plug his head full of lead.*

As far as D'Quandree was concerned, Ferguson would not get the best of him. He was the smartest fucker around and he was going to make sure Ferguson took his last breath on Earth.

Jones sat on an abandoned milk crate and waited. He looked at his Rolex Explorer II Stainless Steel White Dial Men 40 mm Automatic Watch 16570. In five minutes, he would have this revenge. *He thinks he is so smart heading up the Gang Violence Crime Unit. He wants to get rid of all the good guys with a trip to the gray bar hotel. Fuck him! I'll show him how smart he is. I want him to have a good look at me before I blast him into never, never land. He is a piece of shit.*

His heart was pounding the closer it got to Ferguson's arrival, and it felt like his heart was having an out-of-body experience. He looked forward to this assassination and never felt so right about all his crimes.

The train pulled into Clinton Station and Jones stood still by the tall uncut shrubs. He was ready to make his move.

Jones saw Ferguson disembark the train as he began his short walk to his parked 1995 Mercedes-Benz C-Class sedan. Ferguson opened the door and sat in the front seat as he was leaving a message for his wife to let her know he would be home soon.

Jones jumped out of the shrubs, held the car door open, and yelled, "Hey, motherfucker!" He paused. "I'm going to send you to your ancestors."

The first bullet went through Ferguson's left eye, shattering his eyeglasses. Ferguson felt pain at first and then nothing as bullets ripped through his skull and left him slumped dead in his seat, covered in blood. Blood and brain matter had splattered all over Ferguson and his front seat.

Jones looked around to see if anyone heard the shots as he began walking fast to Washington's car. Jones lost his blood-splattered glove and hat running to the car.

He jumped in Washington's car and yelled, "Step on it." They drove a few blocks, and Jones threw the nine-millimeter Beretta semiautomatic handgun into a wooded area.

Police and travelers ran to Ferguson's car once they heard the shots and found Ferguson slumped over his steering wheel covered in blood. First responders telephoned for backup.

Jones and Washington arrived at his apartment and slapped Washington on his back, proudly stating, "We did it! We got rid of that maggot!"

"We did it!" Washington shouted , and he gave Jones a spirited high five.

The dynamic duo downed the first beer with a shot of whiskey.

"Our troubles are over," Jones said. "He won't bother us anymore. We won't have to worry about his gang unit." Jones smiled; confident he was in the clear.

Chapter Twirty

July 12, 1995, 4:30 p.m.

First responders and travelers came running to Ferguson's car once they heard the shots. They found the blood-covered Attorney General slumped over the steering wheel, not breathing. The point-blank shot shattered his eyeglasses. Brain matter and blood covered the dashboard and front seats.

Pictures were taken of Ferguson's motionless body, dashboard, seat, floor, and door of Ferguson's car. The Crime Scene Unit collected samples of blood and brain matter and looked for fingerprints. Fingerprints were found on the car door, but it was unknown at the time if these prints would prove useful for the crime examination.

The Medical Examiner, Sarah Edmunds, wanted the body to be delivered to her office as soon as the Crime Scene Unit completed its examination of the crime scene.

Larry Briggs questioned the first responders to see whether there were any witnesses to the shooting, and they all shook their heads and responded, "No."

"If anyone can remember anything from today, please contact my office," he said as he gave everyone his business card. "We must locate the killer or killers yesterday!" he bellowed.

Ralph Davis was a commuter who parked about forty yards behind Ferguson's car at the Clinton Station on August 21, 1995. His train arrived at the station at 5:30 p.m. After he left the train, he saw Ferguson walking to his car. As he was getting into his car, Davis heard a brief exchange of words and then two shots. He looked up to see an unidentified figure leaning into the driver's side of Ferguson's car.

Davis observed the figure put an object into the back of his pants and flee into the parking lot toward the train tracks. Davis identified the assailant as a twenty to thirty-year-old Black male wearing a black-hooded sweatshirt and baggy jeans but could not specifically identify the person.

"So, you saw this individual run away from Ferguson's car and you cannot identify him?" asked Larry Briggs.

"No, like I told the other officers, I didn't see his face. He was running away from me."

"Okay, please be available for further questioning. You are the only person to see the killer run from Ferguson's car."

"Okay, just give me a call."

Briggs approached a few of the officers at the crime scene and asked if anyone found other witnesses to the shooting. Each one answered in the negative. "Well, continue your search for any clues for this murder."

Chapter Thirty-One

July 12, 1995, Breaking News, 6:00 p.m.

After many beers and shots, the Jones gang turned on the Six O'clock News, and there it was: *"We have breaking news,"* the broadcaster stated. *"Attorney General Alphonse Ferguson has been assassinated gangland-style in his car in the Clinton Station Parking Lot at 5:30 p.m. Commuters thought they heard two or three shots that sounded like firecrackers."*

Just then, the camera pans on Deputy Attorney General Larry Briggs. *"Ferguson succumbed to multiple shots to the head. We will conduct a thorough review, but let me be clear. We will capture the perps and they will pay for this killing.*

"Lieutenant Brianna Watkins, Major Crimes Supervisor, will head up the investigation and we have given her all the resources to bring down the killers as soon as possible. The fine work done by Attorney General Ferguson with his Gang Crime Task Force will continue with me!

"We will release information as it becomes known to us. We welcome any assistance from the public and tips may be called

into our task force. Please call the number on your screen with any information that will lead to identifying the person who committed this heinous murder."

Jones turned the TV off and a round of high fives ensured, expressing that victory was theirs.

Their cries of "The motherfucker is gone," echoed throughout the house.

"Our worries are gone," Jones yelled. "Good work, Washington. My thanks to all you muthafuckas for everything that you have done."

Chapter Thirty-Two

July 12, 1995, 7:30 p.m.

On the night of the murder, Melissa White was at her daughter's apartment when she heard D'Quandree Jones boast, "I don't have to worry no more. I took care of my problem."

Jones bragged that he hid in the bushes and then came out when Ferguson came to his car and shot him twice in the head. When Melissa asked Jones why he had done that, Jones replied, "I don't want to go back to prison and AG Ferguson was going to give me a lot of time for the murder of Jenkins, I knew he was going to try and hang me, but I'm not going out like that." Jones later asked her for money so he could leave town until all the drama quieted down.

Wendy White saw Jones during the evening of Ferguson's murder at Leslie Smith's apartment. At one point, he was soaking his hands in bleach, and she noticed he was not wearing the black-hooded sweatshirt he had on earlier in the day. She heard him say, "I have no more worries and I don't have a prosecutor."

Jones told Harold Haynes the day after the murder that he killed Ferguson because "He was going to give me life on the carjacking case" and Jones did not want to get life. Jones recounted the entire crime to Haynes, explaining that he came out of the bushes and then he fled to a waiting car, losing his sweatshirt, cap, and bandana on the way. Jones said he later asked Washington to get rid of his car, but Washington was stopped by the police, and the car was impounded. Jones threatened Haynes that he would kill him if he "snitched."

Chapter Thirty-Three

History of Chicago Murders—The Next Day

Polansky was reading the *Chicago Times* examination of the murder rate in Chicago, and it reported that homicides soared to nine hundred twenty in 1992, the highest number since 1973. One expert thought, *"The introduction of crack cocaine came at a time when the murder rate shot up." Another expert said,* "The increase in homicides can be explained by an unstable drug market. There was a lot of competition for the crack market from the late 1980*s to the 1990s in the inner-city community and that led to many homicides."* Territory was a major driver of gang violence in the 1990s. The article continued to describe the demolishment of the high-rise public housing projects; people, including gang members, were displaced. This meant drug-selling gang members were forced to live in areas already claimed by other gangs, causing conflicts.

Polansky knew D'Quandree Jones was deeply entrenched in his neighborhood, with little resistance from rival gangs.

Polansky thought, *Jones is the King of the Hill and keeps a tight rein on his territory and his boys.*

Chapter Thirty-Four

Review of the Facts

Police searching the area around Clinton Station found several articles of clothing. Along the railroad tracks, police officers found a black hooded sweatshirt, a left-hand glove, a cap, and a green bandana. They discovered matching glove and knit cap tucked inside the sweatshirt.

Police also recovered a slug from the driver's side of the dashboard of Ferguson's car. They also discovered footprints in an area directly across from his car and a milk crate and discarded cigarette butt. They could not match the footprints to any brand or manufacturer of footwear.

Polansky and Sweeney were glad to get the Crime Scene Unit Report.

Sweeney said, "Now we can begin the work needed to convict Jones. I cannot wait to see the smile on his face when he gets life for this murder. We still have to wait for the ME's report and findings. That should come in a day or so once Sarah Edmunds completes her autopsy of Ferguson and reviews the lab test results. In the meantime, we can begin to pin information on our Crime Analysis Board. We have pictures of Ferguson and Jones, photos from the murder scene, footprints, statements from the Birdsalls."

Sweeney offered the importance of this kind of detective work. "We can't tell you how many murders we have solved just taking a closer look at these boards," he said to Polansky. "Newspaper clippings, notes, maps, specific crime scene details. What clues one person misses, another can piece together to pin the perp."

Chapter Thirty-Five

Chillin'

Deshaun cracked open a can of Bourbon County Stout (Goose Island Beer Co.). "Could there have been any other option? The first imperial stout aged in bourbon barrels debuted at Goose Island's Clybourne Avenue brewpub in 1995. Some people were disturbed by its depth of boozy flavor. Others couldn't believe that their little local brewpub had concocted such liquid gold. The practice of bourbon-barrel aging has since been copied the world over."

He tossed a can to D'Quandree, who cracked the can in record time and guzzled half the can before he gave out a "Whoopee, this is good shit. Man, where'd you get this shit, Deshaun?"

"Member, Lucky went to this bar a few weeks ago, and this is the same shit. Great fuckin' taste. Nothing but the best for you, boss!"

"Muthafucka, this hits the spot. I gotta quit worrying about that scum, Ferguson. He is gone and can't bother me no more. It's time to sit back and enjoy this hot weather. Crank up the air conditioners," Jones yelled.

The house cooled down, and Jones and his crew consumed a case of Bourbon County Stout in the afternoon.

"Any of you hear any shit about the Ferguson murder?" Jones asked. "The fucking streets have been quiet, and no one is talking about it."

"Pay no mind, Dee," Frankie said. "You are in the fuckin' clear. Nothing to worry about. They ain't got nothing on you. Chill, muthafucka."

"Snake Eyes, please come in the other room. I want to talk with you."

"Okay, boss."

"Listen, if for some freakin' reason I'm arrested and found guilty of killing Attorney General Ferguson, please find a way to shoot me. I do not want to go to prison. Can you promise me this?"

"Don't worry. I'll take care of it."

Chapter Thirty-Six

Eclectic Visitor, 8:00 a.m.

Parked at the edge of the park next to the Clinton Station, Uncle Freddy shared with anyone walking by that he had traveled to the forty-eight continental states in his 1979 Chevy SUV.

At first glance, one would swear he was a holdover from the sixties with a Harley Davidson bandana tightly wrapped around his long, unwashed blond hair. He wore peace symbol earrings hanging from each ear and his nose. He wore a tattered Yellowstone National Park t-shirt with ragged, dirty blue jeans, the kind of pants you could stand in the corner of your bedroom waiting to be worn the next morning.

Presently, he was taping a green Sprite can to his front bumper alongside a previously fastened can. When asked, "Why the cans?" He answered, "Green is my favorite color, and they add pizzazz to the front of the vehicle." The SUV was a mobile museum filled with boxes of books, magazines, souvenirs, and sundry items collected from his wanderings.

"I know where everything is located," Uncle Freddie added. He walked around to the tailgate and pointed to cookbooks from all over the US in the bin. "They include the best recipes in every state in 1900.

"I share everything with people whom I meet and find interesting along the way. Especially people who stop and listen to my stories and beliefs. I know all about Area 51, the highly-classified remote detachment of Edwards Air Force Base, within the Nevada Test and Training Range.

"The base's current primary purpose is publicly unknown. However, over the years, it has been the site where the development and testing of experimental aircraft and weapons systems have taken place. There have been many unfounded theories about UFOs and aliens living in Area 51, especially in 1950. The Lockheed U-2 strategic reconnaissance aircraft was developed and tested there.

"The famed SR-71 Blackbird flew its initial flight in 1959 in Area 51. This was the US first stealth aircraft owing to its radar-reflective design. The SR-71's extreme performance was a speed of Mach 3.3 at an altitude of eighty-five thousand feet. It could take a picture of a golf ball at that height and reveal the make of the golf ball very clearly.

"The Blackbird wouldn't stay secret until President Lyndon Johnson would run for election in 1964, and to counter criticisms from Republican Senator Barry Goldwater revealed the SR-71 during a speech on July 25.

"CIA Project OXCART received eight USAF F-101 Voodoos for training, two T-33 Shooting Star trainers for proficiency flying, a C-130 Hercules for cargo transport, a U-3A for administrative purposes, a helicopter for search and rescue, and a Cessna 180 for liaison use; and Lockheed provided an F-104 Starfighter for use as a chase plane in the earlier 1960s.

"I know all about the government's attempt to rule our minds," said Uncle Freddie. "I have been on to their tricks and secrecy for years. Big Brother is in our lives and people don't know it.

"I have also communicated with aliens, and they don't want to reveal themselves for fear of slaughter. They live among us and wish to live in peace."

Chapter Thirty-Seven

July 23, 1995

Sarah Edmunds, Coroner Inspector, called Lieutenant Brianna Watkins and asked her to come to the morgue to discuss Alphonse Ferguson's autopsy. Within the hour, Watkins walked into Edmunds's office.

"Hi, Sarah. How are you doing?" asked Lieutenant Watkins. "I brought Gerry Fontaine, AG Investigator 12 with me."

"Hi, guys. Good to see you. Well, I won't waste any of your time and we all know why you are here. I have the autopsy results for Attorney General Ferguson."

"Great, we've been waiting for this report," Brianna said.

"Well then, let's get right into it:

"Autopsy: Rigor mortis was slightly felt in his extremities. The scleral and conjunctival surface of the left eye are unremarkable. The right eye cannot be accessed due to an acute traumatic injury (gunshot wound).

"Injuries: There is a gunshot entrance wound of the vertex

of the scalp. There is a gunshot entrance wound of the central forehead. There is a gunshot-related defect present near the right eyelid that measures 3.0 x 1.0 cm. There is an abrasion present near the right forehead that measures 3.5 cm in greatest dimension. There is an open wound in back of the head where one of the bullets exited.

"Detailed Description of Specified Injuries:

1. There is a gunshot entrance wound of the vertex of the scalp. The wound is located 20.0 cm above the level of the right external auditory meatus and near midline of the vertex of the head. The hole measures 10 mm x 8 mm. It is round with level edges. The edges focally show an abrasion ring measuring up to 1 mm in greatest dimension and is most prominent near the superior edge of the wound. No powder stipple is identified. No soot identified. The wound track shows deeper hemorrhage. A bullet, seen on x-rays, is found within the soft tissue of the right face and is recovered and submitted as evidence. Evaluation of this wound indicates that it is an entrance wound. The path of this shot is downward and rightward. The track of this bullet has been traced to pass via the scalp, soft tissue, parietal bone of the skull, right parietal lobe of the brain, right temporal bone of the skull to exit in the rear of the head.

2. There is a gunshot entrance wound of the central forehead. This wound is located 7.0 cm above the level of the right external auditory meatus and 2.0 cm right of the anterior midline of the head. The hole measures 15 mm x 10 mm. It is oval with slightly inverted edges. The edges show an abrasion ring measuring up to 3 mm in greater dimension and is most prominent near the superior edge of the wound. X-rays show small bullet fragments associated with this wound; however, due to their small size are not recovered as evidence."

"That follows along the line of our thinking. Thanks for the update. Now we have to find the perp who assassinated Ferguson in close range," replied Brianna. "We'll leave you to your work. Thanks for the information."

"It's my pleasure. See you after the next murder," Sarah said her goodbyes.

Chapter Thirty-Eight

July 24, 1995, Jury Service

After much thought, Charlotte Steele took the commuter train from Overton to Clinton Station. *She would stop at Dunkin Donuts for her morning coffee and muffin and board the train for downtown Chicago. The trip would take forty-five minutes, and she welcomed the opportunity to catch up with the news in her Chicago Tribune.*

The 11:00 a.m. train arrived on time, and Charlotte boarded to the sound of the conductor announcing, "All aboard!"

Small world. The conductor was Roger Paltry, a former customer of hers when she was a bartender. Often, she watched them come into the bar; a frozen daiquiri and draft beer waited for them.

"How's it going, Roger? How is Faith?"

"We are both fine. I haven't seen you in a long time. What are you up to nowadays?"

"I left the restaurant a few years back. Now I'm a freelance writer and I'm on my way to Chicago for jury duty at the Circuit Court of Cook County. Well, it is good seeing you Roger." She gave Roger a hug goodbye.

On her way to her seat, *Charlotte thought back to her days at the bar and remembered all the good customers she had. She was especially fond of Roger and Faith and thoroughly enjoyed their company.*

Chapter Thirty-Nine

August 14, 1996, Trial

Charlotte Steele entered the Circuit Court of Cook County and took the elevator to the fifth floor where she would report to the jury pool. She wondered what this experience would be like. This was the first time that she had jury duty. She realized that this was a big case, the killing of an Attorney General. She reported on time and sat in a room with forty-five other prospective jurors. She wouldn't know who was on trial until she was selected as a juror and received instructions from the judge. A film discussing jury duty played to the group for fifteen minutes. At the completion of the film, a court officer read off twenty names that represented the people picked to be questioned for jury service.

Charlotte moved to the front of the room and proceeded to the court when she heard her name called and waited to be questioned by the lawyers. Charlotte passed the *voir dire* questions with flying colors and was selected as a juror for the murder trial of Attorney General Alphonse Ferguson.

The primary purpose of *voir dire* questioning was to make sure jurors could listen fairly and impartially to the evidence and render a verdict in accordance with the law. However, Charlotte learned from her attorney that the lawyers would try to get a sense of how a juror would respond to the evidence and arguments in the case about to be tried.

Charlotte was one of twelve jurors selected for this trial with two alternates. She took her seat in the first row, sitting closest to Judge Mary Simpson. She would learn the names of the other jurors once they were sent to deliberate the case. She was impressed with the fresh smell of oak in the courtroom.

The racially-mixed jury included seven men and five women.

Two jurors had to be replaced just prior to the start of the trial after they expressed fear for their safety.

The first person Charlotte wanted to see was D'Quandree Jones. He was well dressed in a striped blue suit with a blue tie. He showed no remorse. She couldn't keep her eyes off the accused murderer throughout the trial. He showed no emotion, and his look appeared frozen in time.

The bailiff addressed the court. "Please rise. The Circuit Court of Chicago, Criminal Division, is now in session. The Honorable Mary Simpson is presiding."

Entering the courtroom and taking her seat behind her bench, Judge Simpson had been a Circuit Court Judge since 1988. She was one of three hundred fifty judges on the Circuit

Court. The elected judges stood for retention every six years and they never lost.

Judge Simpson started her legal career as a law clerk and, later, Chief Law Clerk to Supreme Court Justice Frank Abernathy. She joined the Administrative Office of the Illinois Courts (AOIC) in 1991, becoming Chief Legal Counsel for the Administrative Office within three years. She was initially appointed the Director of the AOIC in 1994.

"Good morning, ladies and gentlemen. Calling the case of the People of the state of Illinois versus D'Quandree Jones. Are both sides ready?" Judge Simpson asked. "Is the prosecution ready?"

Prosecutor Ralph Emerson stood up and responded, "Yes, Your Honor," and took his seat.

"Is the defense ready?"

Defense Attorney Clarence Huffington stood up and responded, "Yes, Your Honor," and took his seat.

"Will the clerk please swear in the jury?"

The clerk asked each of the jurors to stand and raise their right hand. "Do each of you swear that you will fairly try the case before this court, and that you will return a true verdict according to the evidence and the instructions of the court, so help you God? Please say 'I do.'"

All the jurors said in unison, "I do."

"You may be seated," the clerk said.

Judge Simpson began her instructions to the jury. "Members of the jury, your duty today will be to determine whether the defendant is guilty or not guilty based only on facts and evidence provided in this case. The prosecution has the burden of proving the guilt of the defendant beyond a reasonable doubt. This burden remains on the prosecution through the trial. The prosecution must prove that a crime was committed, and that the defendant is the person who committed the crime. However, if you are not satisfied of the defendant's guilt to that extent, then reasonable doubt exists, and the defendant must be found not guilty."

Judge Simpson then informed the jury that they were going to take a bus ride the following morning to see all the important sites discussed in this trial. The bus will leave at 10:00 a.m. sharp and it will be parked in front of the courthouse.

"Now, Mr. Emerson, you may proceed with your opening statement," said Judge Simpson.

"Thank you, Your Honor." Emerson got up from the table and walked toward the jury. "Good morning, ladies and gentlemen of the jury. It is my pleasure to represent the State of Illinois and to serve as a prosecutor on this very important case. On July 12, 1995, the defendant in this matter allegedly shot and killed Attorney General Alphonse Ferguson.

"This was a tragic killing of a fine guardian of the law. General Ferguson was relentless in his pursuit of gang activity to provide a safe and secure environment for the citizens of this fine city. It is disgusting to hear of so many deaths of our poor citizens in this severe heat dying because they were afraid to leave their homes. The violence and murder rate must come to an end and that was the sole purpose of General Ferguson's desire to jail all who deserve to be put behind bars.

"Attorney General Ferguson's murder was premeditated and horrific.

"DNA evidence is very powerful. It has firm roots in science and is backed by statistics. Analysts focus on thirteen or more places in the genome, called loci, where humans are extraordinarily diverse. Each locus contains a 'short tandem repeat,' a bit of DNA that is repeated multiple times. The exact number of repeats at each locus varies from person to person and can range anywhere between the low single digits to the mid-fifties. Because we get one copy of each chromosome from our mother and one from our father, there are two numbers for each locus, which appear as peaks on an electropherogram, a chart produced by a genetic analyzer.

"The chance that two people have the same pairs at all thirteen loci is astronomically low. It's a bit like pulling the handles of two slot machines with thirteen cylinders each—all containing dozens of symbols—and hoping they match up right down the line.

"DNA is generally used in one of two ways. In cases where a suspect is identified, a sample of that person's DNA can be compared to evidence from the crime scene. The results of this comparison may help establish whether the suspect committed the crime. In cases where a suspect has not yet been identified, biological evidence from the crime scene can be analyzed and compared to offender profiles in DNA databases to help identify the perpetrator. Crime scene evidence can also be linked to other crime scenes using DNA databases.

"Forensic science is used to help victims of crimes and victims of disasters. Using the polymerase chain reaction (PCR) process can make millions of copies of DNA from just a few skin and hair cells. These DNA techniques can help tie criminals to a crime and victim.

"DNA profiling has become one of the most valuable tools in forensic science. By comparing highly variable regions of the genome in DNA from a sample with DNA from a short distance from the crime scene, detectives can help prove the culprit's guilt – or establish innocence.

"The great advantage of DNA profiling lies in its specificity. Even relative minute quantities of DNA at a crime scene can yield sufficient material for analysis. Forensic scientists typically compare at least 13 markers from the DNA in two samples. In a test with thirteen markers, the probability that any two individuals would have identical profiles is estimated to be below 1 in 10 billion.

"Consequently, when specimens are collected properly, and the procedure is performed correctly, DNA profiling is an extremely accurate way to compare a suspect's DNA with crime scene specimens.

"We will present witnesses and offer DNA investigative results from three different laboratories who tested clothing found at the crime scene. At the conclusion of this case, and after you have heard all the evidence, we are confident that you will return a verdict of guilty in the first degree. The Prosecutor walked back and forth in front of the jury.

"Snake Eyes Washington will testify that he was asked by D'Quandree Jones to follow the Attorney General from his work to his car and report his results to Jones. He will testify that Jones used this information to plan his murder of Attorney General Alphonse Ferguson.

"You'll hear Melissa White comment on how she heard Jones boast, 'I don't have to worry no more. I took care of my problem' when he described how he took care of the Attorney General.

"Harold Haynes will testify that Jones recounted the entire crime to him about how he shot the Attorney General.

"Snake Eyes Washington will share that he drove the defendant to the Clinton Station and waited for him while he committed his crime. Washington also told Jones that he wouldn't snitch on him.

"Ralph Davis will testify that he saw a figure argue with the Attorney General and then he heard two gun shots and saw the AG's legs hanging out his door as the shooter ran out of the parking lot.

"Conclusive DNA investigations from three different laboratories will reveal that the Attorney General's blood was found on several articles of clothing found a short distance from the crime scene.

"All of this witness testimony and DNA evidence will show that the defendant, D'Quandree Jones, is guilty of first-degree murder of Attorney General Alphonse Ferguson.

Members of the jury, thank you for your service."

"Thank you, Mr. Emerson," said Judge Simpson. "We will now have an opening statement from the Defense Attorney Clarence Huffington."

"Thank you, Your Honor. Good morning, ladies and gentlemen of the jury. The death of Attorney General is a tragedy. A loss of a very fine Attorney General who has the executive responsibility for law enforcement, prosecutions or even responsibility for legal affairs generally here in Illinois.

"Your Honor, and ladies and gentlemen of the jury, under the law, my client is presumed innocent until proven guilty. You will come to know the truth: that my client did not commit this crime. My client has had many run-ins with the law, but he is not the person responsible for the death of Attorney General Ferguson. Yes, he has faced Ferguson twice in court and won, but he is not guilty of this murder.

"You will hear many witnesses who claim to hear the defendant brag about this killing, but you will not hear one witness who is able to identify my client as the shooter. I will present witnesses who will rebut what the prosecution's witnesses will tell you. Some of the prosecution's witnesses have had problems with my client and want to railroad him for this crime."

The defense attorney waved his fist in the air and stated emphatically, "The prosecution has been unable to produce one witness who can identify my client as the shooter in this case. Hearsay evidence is inadmissible for lack of a firsthand witness.

"The witness who witnessed General Ferguson's murder cannot identify the defendant as the one who shot General Ferguson.

"While the correct use of DNA can be contributed in reducing and reversing innocent convictions, incorrect use of it and the sway of it over other evidence on juries and judges can produce a system of innocent convictions. However, errors can be made and individuals conducting the tests, possibly, could be convinced through criminal means to produce the desired outcomes. All these problems make DNA profiling a tool with under one hundred percent accuracy.

"DNA evidence is only one of the many types of evidence jurors should consider, when considering a case. TV shows like *CSI* may have popularized forensic science to the point some jurors have unrealistic expectations of DNA analysis and accord it more weight than other types of evidence. This phenomenon is sometimes called the *CSI* effect. Maintaining

DNA databanks can help police identify criminals, but it can also pose ethical quandaries when authorities keep samples from people who have never been accused of any crime.

"Partial profiles will match up with many more people than a full profile. And even full profiles may match with a person other than the culprit. Further complicating matters, a single profile might be mistakenly generated when samples from multiple people are accidentally combined. It's a messy world.

"Realistically, then, DNA profiles should only be thought of as being *likely* to have come from a specific individual. Statistical approaches such as "match probability," which is based on comparisons between crime scene DNA and a hypothetical "random" person, often are misunderstood. A more rigorous approach is likelihood ratio, which directly compares two hypotheses: the likelihood of the DNA coming from the suspect vs. the likelihood of the DNA coming from someone else.

"DNA technology is becoming more and more sensitive, but this is a double-edged sword. On the one hand, usable DNA evidence is more likely to be detected than ever before. On the other hand, contamination DNA and DNA that arrived by secondary transfer is now more likely to be detected, confusing investigations. If legal and judicial personnel aren't fully trained in how to interpret forensic and DNA evidence, it can result in false leads and miscarriages of justice.

"Members of the jury, you will have one decision to make and that is that my client is innocent. Thank you for your service."

Judge Mary Simpson asked the prosecution to call their first witness.

"Thank you, Your Honor. I call to the stand, Melissa White."

"Will the witness please stand to be sworn in by the bailiff?"

Melissa White stood and raised her right hand.

"You do solemnly state that the testimony you may give in the case now pending before this court shall be the truth, the whole truth, and nothing but the truth, so help you, God."

"I do." Melissa White walked to the stand and sat down.

"Mrs. White, what is your relationship to the defendant?"

"I'm just a friend. Everyone knows everyone in the neighborhood."

"Where were you on August 21, 1995, the day of the murder of General Ferguson?"

"I was in Leslie Simpson's apartment the night of the murder when I heard D'Quandree Jones boast, 'I don't have to worry no more. I took care of my problem.'"

"What else did he say?"

"He bragged that he hid in the bushes and then came out when Ferguson came to his car and shot him twice in the head.

"When I asked Jones why he did that, Jones replied, 'He did not want to go back to prison, and that AG Ferguson was going to give me a lot of time.

"Jones further stated, 'I know he is going to try and hang me, but I'm not going out like that!'" Melissa also said that Jones later asked her for money, so that he could leave town.

"I have no further questions for this witness, Your Honor."

Judge Simpson stated the defense attorney could cross-examine the witness.

"Mrs. White, when you allegedly heard these comments from the defendant, were you in the same room as the defendant?" asked Mr. Huffington.

"No."

"Then how do you know it was the defendant that said what you allegedly heard?"

"I just know his voice."

"You say you know his voice, but you weren't in the room when you heard this person speak and you think it was the defendant because you know his voice. It could have been someone else talking. Right, Mrs. White?"

"No, it was the defendant. I know his voice."

"Thank you, Mrs. White. am finished with this witness, Your Honor."

Chapter Forty

August 14, 1996

And so ended the first day of this murder trial of Attorney General Alphonse Ferguson.

"This concludes today's proceedings," said Judge Simpson. "We will meet again tomorrow morning at 9:00 a.m."

Charlotte and the other jurors exited through the side door and maintained judicial silence on their way outside. Once outside, Charlotte headed for the parking lot and went to the fourth floor of the parking garage and got into her car. She felt tired from the long-anticipated trial and wanted to be home so she could undress and take a nice, long shower.

As she was enjoying the water spraying over her body, Charlotte looked back on the day and was glad she was on this jury. *This is going to be an interesting trial and I look forward to hearing all the evidence and witnesses.* Although the judge said jurors could not take notes during the trial, she thought it would be good for her to take notes at home to help her remember the details of the trial. After copious note taking,

Charlotte had a quick meal and stretched on her bed and watched the latest news. Sleep came fast.

The alarm signaled day two of the trial and Charlotte went through her morning routine quickly and wanted to get to court on time. She got to the courthouse in time to join the other jurors on a bus to visit the different sites of the crime.

Ralph Emerson, the Prosecutor, addressed the group and let them know they were going to follow Attorney General Alphonse Ferguson on his last day on Earth.

"Our first stop will be the James R. Thompson Center, where his office is located."

The glass and steel structure's open floor plan and massive open atrium were intended to be architectural metaphors for transparency and open government in action. The sculpture at the front entrance by French artist Jean Dubuffet had set the tone for this building that housed a tremendous art collection.

"Mr. Ferguson walked to the Clark/Lake Station on the Blue Line to travel fifteen minutes to the Clinton Station," said Prosecutor Emerson.

Clinton Station was the last underground station on the Dearborn Street Subway, although it opened with the line in the median of the Eisenhower Expressway in 1958, not in 1951 when the rest of the subway opened, with LaSalle as the temporary southern terminus. The stop was the closest 'L' station to Union Station, located two blocks north and one block west of the station. Signs on the mezzanine direct passengers here (with Amtrak, Pace, Metra, and CTA logos) and to the Greyhound station a block south and two east.

Entering the station, passengers reached a tiny little mezzanine with mostly original, gray cinder-block-sized tile walls. There was light blue text for the various sides of Clinton Station before turnstiles, next to an original cashier's booth which led to a double set of single-person- size escalators and a staircase down to near the eastern end of an island platform that was deep underground. This island platform had the usual white arch roof with a line of fluorescent lights embedded in it. There were similar arches along the dark tracks. Signage was unique, with illuminated Clinton Station signs in a modern-looking font hanging from the ceiling in blue fixtures. This complimented pillar signs and hard-to-see track wall signs opposite the platform. Similar tiled pillars were along the escalators up to leave the platform and Clinton/Congress was written in light blue on the tiles.

The bus pulled into the parking lot at the Clinton Station and drove toward the site where AG Alphonse Ferguson parked his car and where he was shot. "Over there are the bushes that D'Quandree Jones allegedly hid waiting for the arrival of the AG from work. You can then follow his run down the tracks to a waiting car driven by Snake Eyes Washington. This also marks the trail of clothes that Jones left behind.

"Two rows to the left is where Ralph Davis was parked when he saw the shooting."

"Any questions?" asked the formally-attired prosecutor.

"Yeah," said one of the jurors in the back of the bus. "Were the clothes Jones discarded tested for DNA evidence?"

"As a matter of fact, they were, and they will be key elements in the trial.

"If there are no more questions, we'll head back to the courthouse," said Emerson.

Once they returned to the courthouse, the prosecutor excused the jurors and reminded them to return to court at 9:00 a.m. tomorrow.

Chapter Forty-One

August 15, 1996, Back at Court, 9:00 a.m.

"Your Honor, I'd like to call my next witness, Ms. Wendy White," said Prosecutor Emerson.

"Will the witness stand to be sworn in by the bailiff?" asked Judge Simpson.

"You do solemnly state that the testimony you may give in the case now pending before this court shall be the truth, the whole truth, and nothing but the truth, so help you God."

"I do."

"Please state your first and last name."

"Wendy White."

Clerk said, "Thank you. You may be seated."

"Ms. White, please tell the court what you saw during the evening of the murder of Attorney General Ferguson on August 21, 1995," said Prosecutor Ralph Emerson.

"I saw the defendant during the evening of the Attorney General's murder at Leslie Smith's apartment. At one point, he was soaking his hands in bleach, and I wondered why he was doing this. I noticed that he was not wearing his black-hooded sweatshirt that he had on earlier in the day."

"What did you hear him say?"

"I hear him say that he had no more worries and that he did not have a prosecutor."

"You saw him earlier in the day? About what time?"

"I don't remember exactly. Maybe noon time."

"And he was wearing his black-hooded sweatshirt then?"

"Yes."

"The defense may cross-examine the witness."

"Ms. White, how do you know Mr. Jones?"

"He lives near me."

"How long have you known him?"

"As long as I can remember."

"Why did you remember that my client was no longer wearing a black-hooded sweatshirt the night of July 12, 1995? Do you have a habit of keeping close tabs with people with what they are wearing?"

"Well, no."

"Well then, why did you remember what my client was not wearing on that night in question?"

"I don't know. I just did."

"Why do you think that he was washing his hands with bleach?"

"I have no idea."

The Prosecutor addressed the Judge. "Your Honor, I would like to bring my next witness to the stand, Harold Haynes."

"You do solemnly state that the testimony you may give in the case now pending before this court shall be the truth, the whole truth, and nothing but the truth, so help you God."

"I do."

"What is your first and last name?"

"Harold Haynes"

"Mr. Haynes, what relation are you to the defendant?"

"He is my dawg."

"What do you mean?"

"He is my friend."

"So, he is your friend?"

"Yes."

"What did the defendant say to you on July 13, 1995, the day after the murder of Attorney General Ferguson?"

"Jones told me about the day after the murder that he killed Ferguson, saying "He was going to give me life on the carjacking case" and Jones did not want to get life.

"He said this to you?"

"Jones told the entire crime to me, explaining that he came out of the bushes, shot the Attorney General, and fled to a waiting car, losing his sweatshirt, cap, and bandana on the way."

"He said this to you?"

"Yes."

"Why do you think he told this story to you?"

Jones said he later asked Washington to get rid of his car, but Washington was stopped by the police and the car was impounded. Jones threatened to kill me if I 'snitched' and I know he meant that.

"I don't know. He just did."

"Thank you, Mr. Haynes."

"Mr. Huffington, you may cross-examine the witness," said Judge Simpson.

"Mr. Haynes, how do you know the defendant?" pried the Defense Attorney.

"I live near him, and he is my homeboy. I chill with him. I'll go to his house, or he'll come see me and have a few beers and a few laughs."

"Mr. Haynes, why do you think the defendant would tell you about allegedly killing the Attorney General?"

"I don't know. I knew that he didn't like the AG, but I didn't think that his negatude would lead him to this murder."

"Allegedly," said the dapper defense attorney. "My client allegedly told you not to snitch and here you are testifying at his trial. Aren't you afraid something will happen to you?"

"Listen, all I know is that he told me those things. I'm not saying he did it. This is what he said to me." Mr. Haynes quivered.

"Thank you, Mr. Haynes."

"Your Honor, I call my next witness to the stand, Snake Eyes Washington," stated the Prosecutor.

Judge Simpson asked the witness to stand to be sworn in by the bailiff.

"Please raise your right hand. Do you promise that the testimony you shall give in the case before this court shall be the truth, the whole truth, and nothing but the truth, so help you God?"

"I do." Washington walked to the stand and sat down.

"Please state your first and last name."

"Snake Eye Washington."

"What is your first name?"

"Harold."

"Thank you. What is your relationship with the defendant?"

"We are tight. We chill in his crib or around the neighborhood."

"Where were you on July 12, 1995, the day the Attorney General was murdered?"

"I was with Ree. I took him to Union Station to visit a friend."

"Did you leave him there?"

"Yes."

"What happened next?"

"I saw Jones the next day and asked him about the murder. Jones told me, 'Don't worry about it, don't say fuckin' nothing and if anybody asks, I never asked you to follow Ferguson and never say anything about it.'

"About a month after the shooting, Jones asked me, 'You wouldn't turn me over for $50,000? You wouldn't try to snitch or anything like that against me?' I assured him that I would not be, that I was loyal."

"Thank you, Mr. Washington."

Mr. Huffington began his cross-examination, asking the witness why he thought the defendant allegedly murdered the Attorney General?

"I dunno, but he had me follow the dude from his work to the train station until he got off at Clinton Station. It was the same muthafucka that was investigating gang attacks."

"Please, watch your language!"

"Okay, sorry."

"When the defendant ran to your car at Clinton Station and got into your car, what do you think he was running from?"

"I don't know. He didn't tell me. He just said gun it."

Judge Simpson excused the jury as she reminded them not to discuss the case with each other or with anyone else once they left the courthouse.

Chapter Forty-Two

August 15, 1996

So ended day two of the trial.

D'Quandree Jones couldn't sit still while he waited for his dapper attorney, Clarence Huffington, to appear. Once Huffington came through the door, Jones immediately delivered a barrage. "The muthafucka turned on me and gave me up. What the fuck are you going to do to help me? These muthafuckin' so-called friends are turning on me!"

"You gotta take it easy," assured Huffington. "Your trial just began, and we have time to turn things around. You have to relax."

"'Relax?' I'm on trial for my motherfuckin' life and you tell me to relax? I will not rot in a jail cell!"

With that, Huffington left Jones sitting with his hands and legs shackled and losing hope.

Chapter Forty-Three

August 15, 1996, Return Home

Charlotte politely said, "Goodbye," to some of her fellow jurors and wished them a "Goodnight" as she left the courthouse and headed to her car. While driving home, she reflected on her day. It *seems like the evidence is building against the defendant, but we have a whole trial to cover, with more witnesses and evidence to be presented.*

The sultry juror got her mail and entered her apartment. She took off her shoes, blouse and her bra with exacting speed and relief as the naked investigator poured herself a glass of wine and headed to her living room balcony and surveyed the skyline of Chicago. It was this view that prompted her to take this apartment.

Charlotte was glad that she defrosted the meatballs for her dinner. She heated the tomato sauce made from her mother's recipe. She loved the smell of the meatballs frying in the pan. She made a salad yesterday and added this to her meal. She then played classical music on her Philips F883 made in 1988.

She treasured her aloneness as she slowly enjoyed her meal. Charlotte's life was full of people, and she enjoyed her independence and her home. As she tasted each meatball, memories rush in about her past and wonderful family meals back home in Massachusetts.

The meal finished, and the dishes carefully placed in the dishwasher, the tired juror found solace on her recliner, watching old reruns to help lull her to sleep.

Chapter Forty-Four

August 16, 1995, Day Three of the Trial

"Your Honor, I would like to call my next witness, Ralph Davis," stated the Prosecutor.

"You do solemnly state that the testimony you may give in the case now pending before this court shall be the truth, the whole truth, and nothing but the truth, so help you God."

"I do."

"Please tell me your first and last name."

"Ralph Davis."

Mr. Davis, what were you doing on July 12, 1995, around 5:30 p.m.?"

"I got off the train at Clinton Station at 5:30 p.m. and I walked to my car and I noticed that I was about fifty yards parked behind the Attorney General's car."

"How do you know the Attorney General?"

"I see him on the news on TV."

"Okay, go on."

I saw him walk to his car. As he was getting into his car, I heard a brief exchange of words and then two shots. I looked up to see an unidentified figure leaning into the driver's side of Ferguson's car and Ferguson's legs were hanging out through the open driver's door."

"What did you do next?"

"I observed the figure put an object into the back of his pants and flee into the parking lot toward the exit."

"Can you recognize this person?"

"I would say he was a twenty to thirty-year-old Black male wearing a black-hooded sweatshirt and baggy jeans, but I could not specifically identify the person."

"Thank you, Mr. Davis."

Clarence Huffington, Jones' attorney, cross-examined Ralph Davis and asked him if he could identify the person who shot Ferguson. "Is that person in this court?"

"I cannot say," replied Davis.

"Do you know what this person placed in the back of his pants?"

"I cannot say."

"So, you cannot recognize the person that was outside of the Attorney General's car that night. You don't know what he or she placed in the back of their pants. Then why are you here? I have no more questions."

The prosecution then called Doctor Jonas Spring, the former director of Brackdon Laboratories.

"You do solemnly state that the testimony you may give in the now pending case before this court shall be the truth, the whole truth, and nothing but the truth, so help you God."

"I do."

"Please tell me your first and last name."

"Doctor Jonas Spring."

"Doctor Spring, please explain what you did at Brackdon Laboratories?"

"I directed the operations at the laboratory. I supervised the staff and coordinated the efforts to maintain the accuracy of the operations."

"Doctor Spring, please explain the DNA investigative process."

"Sure, since the advent of DNA testing in 1985, biological material- including skin, hair, blood and other bodily fluids has emerged as the most reliable physical evidence at a crime scene, particularly those involving sexual assaults. DNA, or deoxyribonucleic acid, contains the complex genetic blueprint that distinguishes each person. Forensic testing can determine if distinctive patterns in the genetic material found at a crime scene matches the DNA in a potential perpetrator with better than 99% accuracy. *In 1987, Florida rapist Tommie Lee Andrews became the first person in the U.S. to be convicted be of DNA evidence; he was sentenced to 22 years behind bars.*

"We have ten years of experience of processing difficult samples from all types of crimes. Our clients include prosecutors, law enforcement agencies, defense attorneys, private investigators, hospitals, innocence projects and private individuals, with third-party representation. Our case work services include violent crimes, cold cases, and post-conviction cases. We provide fast turnaround times to meet investigative needs."

"Doctor Spring, please describe your DNA test results that were found at the crime scene," asked the prosecutor.

"We were given a black-hooded sweatshirt, a pair of gloves, a yellow bandana and a knit cap. We performed the first DNA testing and examined various blood stains at six different genetic makers and found a match between the blood found on the garments as Ferguson's blood found at the scene. The likelihood of a random person having this type of genophile was estimated between one in twelve thousand and one in nineteen thousand, dependent on the race used for comparison. Having confirmed that the garments were linked to the alleged murder, additional tests were conducted to determine a profile of the wearer.

"Based on testing of the 'friction' areas, where the wearer of a garment potentially can leave skin cells at points where it rubs against the body. We found DNA material on the collar and right sleeve of the sweatshirt that were consistent with each other. We determined also that the samples contained a mixture of DNA from one or more persons. Currently, we did not have a known sample from Mr. Jones with which to compare the findings. However, after reviewing Jones's genetic profile just prior to the trial, Jones could not be excluded as a donor of the samples recovered from the sweatshirt."

Charlotte was thinking she got more than she bargained for with this trial. She felt she had to pay attention to this discussion about DNA. It was very technical, but it was important to prove whether the accused was at the murder scene.

Prosecutor Emerson continued the questioning of Doctor Spring and asked the former director, "What else did you find from your investigation of the DNA?"

"Further, based on a statistical analysis, the DNA profile found on the sweatshirt would occur randomly in one out of eight hundred to one out of four hundred African Americans."

On cross-examination by Clarence Huffington, Doctor Spring conceded that, "I had been asked to go beyond normal laboratory protocol to determine if there was any detectable DNA evidence whatsoever on the crime scene garments, regardless of whether the quality was sufficient to meet the threshold for testing. I acknowledge that a similar practice by Brackdon resulted in their test results being excluded in a case."

"Doctor Spring, the evidence from your reamplification of the DNA is unreliable. They provide unreliable match frequencies. What say you?"

"We had two tests, one in March and the other in April. I would submit that we had problems with the April testing with reamplification and it had flaws. However, we contend that the March testing had reliable results and we stand behind them."

"Doctor Spring, your database included testing documents of thirteen hundred people. Yet you only provided my client less than one percent of this documentation. What can we do to get a more representative sample?"

"In order to provide you with a complete set of documents, I estimated that production would cost $300,000, and the state said that such an undertaking would take at least two to three months, followed by a similar period for the defense analysis. The state does not dispute the relevance of the requested documents, only the practicality of producing them."

"I have no further questions for this witness."

The prosecution then called Keith Anderson, Deputy Special Agent, Chicago Division for the FBI.

"You do solemnly state that the testimony you may give in the case now pending before this court shall be the truth, the whole truth, and nothing but the truth, so help you God."

"I do."

"Please tell me your first and last name."

"Deputy Special Agent Keith Anderson, Chicago Division for the FBI."

"Mr. Anderson, please tell the court the results you had with analyzing the crime scene evidence.

Deputy Special Agent reported that they "Used a method known as polymerase chain reaction (PCR) and determined that the DNA pattern for blood on the bandana matched that of Ferguson such that only one in 2.3 million Caucasians would have that profile. The left glove also had visible blood stains, but yielded inconclusive results from mixture samples with potentially multiple donors. We did find a small piece of human biological material caught inside the left glove and determined that Jones was the potential major contributor to that DNA, although that too had a mixed pattern. The likelihood of finding such a pattern at random in the African American population was one in four hundred eighty."

"Did you investigate any other crime scene evidence?"

"Yes, the right glove also had very small bloodstains, visible only with the use of enhancement equipment. These stains did not yield strong results, but neither Ferguson nor Jones could be excluded from the mixed DNA patterns discovered there with random match probabilities of one in 85 for African Americans and one in 55 for Caucasians.

"We also determined that Ferguson was a potential donor of a bloodstain on the front of the sweatshirt with the same statistical likelihood as the blood on the bandana. Jones could not be excluded as a donor to a mixed stain found on the collar of the sweatshirt, but the other potential suspects in the case were excluded.

"Our testing also indicated that there were some other potential donor to that sample that we were unable to type. Similar results were obtained from friction areas of the knit cap," Agent Anderson concluded.

"Your Honor, we are finished with this witness."

Chapter Forty-Five

August 17, 1995, Day three is ended

Charlotte briskly left the courthouse and took a cab to Brassiere Jo, one of her favorite stops. She entered the restaurant and walked near the bar and saw someone waving to her. She walked toward the woman only to find out it was her friend, Heather Frost, her favorite weather person.

"What are you doing here, Heather?"

"I could ask you the same question." She hugged Charlotte. "Whenever I'm in the city, I like to stop here for a drink and a bite to eat."

"I came here for the same reason. Let's get a table and catch up on old times."

"Okay, that would be a terrific idea."

Charlotte caught the attention of the hostess, Monique. "Could we get a table over there near the window?

"Come this way," said Monique as she led them to a table with its white tablecloth and a warm glow from the candle.

Once seated, the old friends grabbed the menus and started talking without looking at what the night's specials were.

"Thanks for your help with the information on that tragic heat wave we had," said Charlotte.

"Were you able to write that article?"

"Yes, I did, and it helped a lot. "It is so good to see you."

Charlotte felt a strange feeling come over her at the sight of her friend. She always enjoyed her company when they met, but tonight was different. Heather was wearing a blue summer dress covered with birds that came to the top of her full breasts. She looked sexy tonight, and it produced a tingle in Charlotte.

"Same here."

"You look fabulous tonight, Heather," Charlotte stumbled. She had never found herself attracted to a woman before, but tonight was different."

"Well, thanks Charlotte." Heather blushed. "How was your day? What are you doing recently?"

"Well, you know that murder of Attorney General Alphonse Ferguson a while back?"

"Yeah, I do."

"Well, believe it or not, I'm on the jury for that trial. We just finished our third day in deliberations."

"Wow! That must be fascinating!"

"It is, and I am learning so much about witnesses and DNA evidence. I cannot discuss the case with you, but it is interesting. Let's look at the menu and they have special meals for two. My eye caught the Carotte à la Jo with Michigan Green Asparagus Salad, Ravigote Vinaigrette Filet of Salmon, French Braised Lentils du Puy Parmentier and Chocolate Mousse and a French baguette for dessert."

"That sounds delicious. Let's order it."

"Okay." Charlotte called the waitress and gave her the order.

"Sure. Would you like something from the bar?"

They both agreed on Sauvignon Blanc.

The two old friends went on updating each other about their lives. Charlotte had forgotten how blue Heather's eyes were and she loved her brown hair ending at her elbows. Charlotte was getting more titillated with each glass of wine and mouthful of food.

After paying the bill, they reached the door and exited to the street and felt the warm summer month as the soft wind blew their hair all around.

Charlotte turned to Heather and invited her to her apartment for a nightcap. "My apartment is a short drive—" She stopped mid-sentence when Heather gave her a tight hug and turned her head around for a soft kiss.

"I guess you were feeling the same vibes as me?" asked Charlotte as she closed her eyes and kissed Heather again. The pair were lip locked as Chicago passed them by.

They reached Charlotte's car and immediately lunged for each other, hungering for each other's lips. This went on for a few minutes until Charlotte suggested they head for her apartment. Charlotte put her arm around Heather as Heather leaned into her.

It was a quick ride to the apartment. Charlotte felt the shape of Heather's body as she moved into her and pushed Heather against the wall of the elevator. Once they reached the apartment, Charlotte opened the door and blouses, bras, skirts, panties, and shoes went flying everywhere as they ran into the bedroom.

Once on the bed, Charlotte cupped Heather's breasts and kissed each one as Heather moaned with each kiss. They disappeared into each other's arms and legs.

For Charlotte, this was one of the best moments of her life, and why had she waited so long to be with a woman?

Charlotte kissed Heather's cheeks and lips, moving her hand down her body over her lovely breasts to the tummy and between her legs. She entered her pussy and felt for her clit. Once there, she stroked slowly and felt the warm liquid appearing with each stroke, as Heather's body twisted right and left and up and down. Charlotte continued the stroking until Heather exploded with a wonderful climax and a burst of moans as her body shook with delight.

"That was wonderful, Charlotte. Let me do the same for you" and she outlined Charlotte's body with her hands and followed the curve of her body down to her clitoris. Soon Charlotte was experiencing a feeling she had never had before. Heather hit her sexual fun button.

"I'm glad we met tonight," Charlotte whispered in her ear. "You have a beautiful body, and it feels so good next to mine. I would like you to spend the night" as sleep came to the lovers wrapped around each other.

The alarm woke the couple at 6:30 a.m. and they smiled at each other as they lip locked again. Charlotte stroked Heather's long hair and felt Heather's hand in her vagina again. Charlotte had been with several men, but never experienced the full sexual experience as she had with Heather. Charlotte moved down Heather's body with wet kisses and reached her happy place. She spread Heather's legs and used her tongue to find her clit. She licked softly and enjoyed the sweet taste of Heather's clit juice, which felt like liquid gold.

Charlotte looked at the time and separated from Heather and exclaimed that she had to get ready for the fourth day of deliberations. She grabbed Heather's hands and helped her to her feet. Charlotte felt rushed and apologized profusely that she had to go.

"You may stay in my apartment, and we can spend the weekend together if you like. Mi casa, su casa."

Charlotte admired Heather's nakedness and felt unhappy that she had to leave this beauty, but she thought of a full weekend of sexual excitement with her.

Charlotte hugged and kissed Heather as she rushed for the door and the quick ride to the courthouse.

Chapter Forty-Six

August 18, 1995, DNA Friday

"Your Honor, our next witness is Doctor Carl Jeffries, a Representative for DNA Diagnostics Center."

"You do solemnly state that the testimony you may give in the case now pending before this court shall be the truth, the whole truth, and nothing but the truth, so help you God."

"I do."

"Doctor Jeffries, the Commonwealth sent the same crime scene clothing to you for your analysis?" the prosecutor asked. "You were the third laboratory to investigate possible DNA results."

"We used a type of PCR-based technology known as short tandem repeat (STR) testing. We performed two different sets of testing. First, using DNA extracted from the collar of the sweatshirt, we performed STR analysis in December 1999. This study returned interpretable results at five of the eight genetic locations that were tested. On the basis of the results, it is my opinion that the DNA pattern from the samples found on the sweatshirt matched D'Quandree Jones and appeared at random at a rate of one in 631,000 in the African American population. The statistical opinion arising from the five genetic loci identified during the January testing constitutes the extent of my testimony concerning the sweatshirt sample."

"So, you are saying that Mr. Jones' DNA was present on the sweatshirt?"

"Yes."

Clarence Huffington cross-examined Doctor Jeffries and elicited testimony.

"A second set of testing performed by us in March 1998 yielded results at all eight genetic locations. The March testing suffered from two distinct methodological weaknesses. First, there was evidence that the March testing showed extra fluorescence that potentially indicated contamination in the process used to amplify the DNA. I interpret the results of these tests as containing "artifact," meaning the false indication of an allele that was not present, rather than contamination that would affect the results. I also concede that my laboratory protocol called for the re-extraction and new testing of samples that show evidence of contamination."

Doctor Jeffries further testified that the March testing was subjected to a process known as reamplification. "In order to observe accurately the pattern contained in a given sample, the STR method of testing requires amplification, a process by which enzymes are used to stimulate the DNA to replicate itself. Reamplification is a repetition of this initial process that aims to identify patterns from a small amount of original DNA," D. Jeffries finished.

Mr. Huffington faced Judge Simpson. "I have finished with this witness, Your Honor. I would like to call Deputy Attorney Larry Briggs to the stand."

"You may call the witness."

After being sworn in, Mr. Huffington told Mr. Briggs that he wanted to question Illinois's top lawman about how the evidence was collected from his client, specifically the cigarette butts and drink can consumed in the detective's office when his client was initially questioned.

"Where did you obtain my client's cigarette butts and drink can?"

"We took the cigarette butts and drink can out of the trash can once the defendant left the detective's office to make a phone call to his mother from a secure line in another room of the building," answered Briggs. As a matter of fact, your client did not attempt to take the cigarette butts and drink can when he left the detective's office, and he did not request to go back and collect them after using the telephone, even when prompted. The detectives waited one-half hour before collecting the items to allow Jones an opportunity to return or protest."

Judge Simpson ruled that Jones had no subjective expectation of privacy compelled not by a finding that he legally abandoned them as much as it is by his wholesale failure to manifest any expectation of privacy in the items whatsoever. "Furthermore, there was no error in the denial of Jones' motion to suppress physical evidence as no search or seizure occurred," Judge Simpson finished.

"My client also challenges the introduction of statements he made to police on the day after Ferguson's murder without the benefit of Miranda warnings," Huffington told Briggs.

"Your client was brought to the police station by two plain-clothed officers from his neighborhood when they received information that homicide detectives were interested in speaking with him because he was scheduled to go on trial against Ferguson. He was interviewed by two detectives who asked him if it was okay to tape the interview. Jones replied, 'Do it. I got nothing to hide or worry about.'"

Charlotte found it hard to concentrate on the trial. All she could think about was last night's lovemaking with Heather. She couldn't get home fast enough.

"Jones also acknowledged on the tape that he came to the interview willingly and voluntarily," continued Briggs. "When the interview was over, Jones listened to the tape and was given an opportunity to make corrections before the two homicide detectives gave him a ride back to his neighborhood."

"I object, Your Honor. My client did not receive a Miranda warning prior to being interviewed that day!" said Huffington.

"Your objection is noted."

"If I may, Your Honor," asked Briggs from the witness stand. "I'd like to shed some light on this. Your client was not coerced in this interview. In considering whether a defendant is in police custody, we take into account the following factors: (1) the place of the interrogation; (2) whether officers have conveyed to the person being questioned any belief or opinion that the person is a suspect; (3) the nature of the interrogation, including whether the interview was aggressive or informal; (4) whether, at the time the incriminating statement was made, the person was free to end the interview."

"Jones was interviewed in a detective's office with the door open. The interview was cordial and at no time did Jones request an attorney or ask to leave at any point in the interview."

The judge excused the jury for the day, and they filed out of the courtroom and made their way to the exit. Judge Simpson warned the jurors against discussing the case outside of the courtroom, yet the chatter on the way out was about the enormous amount of DNA evidence that had been presented and they will need to understand what all this meant when they deliberate.

Chapter Forty-Seven

August 18, 1995, End of Day 4

Charlotte made her way to her car and was glad she was on her way home. She thought there was a lot to digest the past week about DNA. She looked forward to deliberations to find her way through all of this chatter. She also couldn't wait to see Heather again.

Her thoughts carried her all over the place until she realized she was home. As she walked to her door, she was greeted with a hug and kiss from her newfound lover.

"I am so glad to see you again. I couldn't wait to get back home with you." They shared a glance of the sky and found it to be very blue with a spackle of wispy clouds outlining the horizon.

Heather was wearing one of Charlotte's T-shirts and a thong. Charlotte couldn't believe that this beauty was in her apartment, and she looked forward to a weekend of food and hot sex.

Heather quickly helped Charlotte out of her clothes and pulled her back to the bedroom.

"You have had a busy day at the courthouse, and I want to take care of you." They were both naked. "Roll over on your stomach," Heather said with an air of sexual command. She sat on Charlotte's butt cheeks and slowly moved her honey pot slowly up and down. She poured Nivea essentially enriched body lotion over the small of her back and rubbed it in as Charlotte felt a stirring between her legs and let out a small moan.

Heather continued to work her way around Charlotte's back as she leaned closer to her and covered her back and shoulders, massaging as she worked her way around Charlotte's body. Heather then asked Charlotte to roll over on her back and she lay on her body, kissing her breasts and then her lips.

They were lip locked and Charlotte loved the warm feeling of Heather's body next to her. After a wonderful hug, Heather began pouring the body lotion on Charlotte's breast and massaged them, tenderly caressing her nipples. Heather continued down Charlotte's welcome body and moved her fingers and then lips up and down her clit.

Charlotte couldn't contain herself and began thrashing up and down in ecstasy, producing a flow of orgasmic liquid over Heather's face to her delight. Charlotte pulled Heather up to kiss her and taste the warm liquid. They laid in bed and continued to discover each other's bodies with kisses.

"I'm going to start the shower and I'd like you to join me," Charlotte said.

"I will join you."

The ladies enjoyed the soap and water as they bathed each other. Once clean, they dried off and got dressed.

"Let's order in, okay?"

"That would be wonderful, Charlotte."

Charlotte ordered supper from her favorite restaurant, The Village Restaurant, and she ordered Veal Marsala "Scallopine with Marsala wine, fresh mushrooms, served over Capellini for two. The order would arrive in twenty minutes and while they waited, she played soft jazz music, and the lovers sipped white wine.

Once the food arrived, Charlotte was intoxicated with the aroma of her dinner, and she thoroughly enjoyed every bite. The food reminded her of her last trip to Salerno, Italy, when she ate at Donato II Marcellaio—Bistrot delle Carni. That dinner was outstanding and so was the company she had with the director of the *Castello di Arechi* ("Arechis' Castle") to discuss an article on the castles of Europe.

Fully satisfied from the meal, they headed back to bed and went to sleep.

Morning came and Charlotte gazed at Heather, who was still sleeping. Her hair was spread out over her pillow. She couldn't believe this beauty was laying in her bed. She thoroughly enjoyed last night and looked forward to a full day with her new lover. She never thought she would find love again.

Heather woke up and turned to hug Charlotte. "Good morning, my love," she whispered. "It is heavenly to wake next to you. I love my body next to you and I feel a lot of love for you."

While Charlotte thought it was rather soon to be talking about love, she couldn't help but have the same feelings for Heather. "Good morning to you," said Charlotte between kisses. "Let's get up and I'll make us a delicious omelet with coffee."

"That sounds great," Heather said as she put on a T-shirt and went to the bathroom.

Charlotte headed for the kitchen, wearing an oversized Chicago Bears shirt. She gathered all the ingredients for their breakfast and started cooking while gazing at her new lover.

"You are a godsend, Heather. You have jump started my life and for that I am grateful."

"I feel the same about you. Imagine, we have been friends for years, but never connected like this. I am glad we ran into each other. Who said there are no coincidences?"

While eating their breakfast, Charlotte asked Heather what she would like to do today.

"I don't know. We could hang out here for a while and discover more about each other."

"That sounds great."

After placing the dishes in the dishwasher, they headed for the living room and settled on the couch in each other's arms.

"Where have you been all my life?" Charlotte asked Heather.

"I'm here now." She held Charlotte's chin and placed soft kisses on her lips.

They fell into the soft cushions of the couch and napped for a while.

Once awake, Charlotte suggested they shower and get dressed and head out to see the windy city.

Heather borrowed Charlotte's clothes, and she picked a white blouse with khaki pants.

"Heather, you look good. Let's go."

They left the building and started walking up the street. Before long, they were at the Chicago River.

They walked for a while and came to the Magnificent Mile, one of the great avenues of the world at the center of all that made Chicago an international destination. They window-shopped for an hour or so at the many stores, restaurants, and hotels. They decided to dine at Café Spiaggia and ordered gnocchi.

"This is an excellent restaurant. Have you been here before?" asked Heather.

"I have, and I wanted to share the experience with you," added Charlotte. "The Magnificent Mile is simply amazing.

It's one of the top ten hospitality, dining and retail destinations in the world, with endless shopping, international cuisine, top rated hotels, lively entertainment, majestic architecture and natural beauty at every turn. People from all over come to visit Chicago's one-of-a-kind city experience.

"There are more than four hundred sixty stores, it's a girl's dream. Not to mention the hundreds of restaurants, hotels, and unique entertainments and attractions packed and stacked along its length—it is quite the indulgence for every passion and every pocket." Charlotte smiled at Heather. "Everything about this place is exceptional. Especially you."

"You're right. It is an amazing place, and you have given me a romantic wake-up call. I never thought I would meet someone like you."

Well, it is settled. After all these years of friendship, we have moved to the next level. I am so glad you ran into me the other night. Let's toast to us."

"To us!"

Charlotte took care of the bill and they exited the restaurant and caught a cab back to Charlotte's apartment.

After Charlotte gave the cabbie the directions, they lip locked in the back seat.

"I hate to interrupt you ladies, but this is your stop," said the cabbie, causing the lovers to unlock.

"Oh, thank you," said Heather as she paid the fare.

They made a dash for the elevator and couldn't wait to get to the apartment.

Once inside the apartment, Charlotte shared that she was very happy. "I had a wonderful day with you, Heather."

"The feeling is mutual," she said, as they quickly unclothed each other and jumped into bed. They continued to probe each other sexually and experienced orgasms never experienced before.

Exhausted from a busy day, the lovers, entangled with each other, fell asleep.

Chapter Forty-Eight

August 19, 1995, Visit Art Institute

The alarm rang at 9:00a.m. and Charlotte turned toward Heather and gave her a soft kiss to start the day. Both wore T-shirts and their panties. They stretched and made their way to the kitchen and began making coffee and pancakes with bacon.

"I love the smell of coffee in the morning," Heather said. "What kind of coffee do you use?"

"Kenya AA Coffee. I get it online."

"It is delicious."

"It is. It has a brilliant acidity with a natural progression of flavors from grapefruit, orange, blackberry, finishing with sublime wine grape, currant flavor, which I love. I also learned that Green Kenyan coffee beans differ from other African varieties because they are often double processed. As a result, they retain a richer, berry flavor with a dry, acidic aftertaste reminiscent of a full-bodied wine."

"Well, aren't you the coffee connoisseur?"

"I love coffee. What would you like to do today?"

"I would love to go to the Art Institute of Chicago and to see their amazing exhibit of Claude Monet, 1840 to 1926, the largest retrospective of his paintings ever assembled. They are expecting huge crowds."

"That sounds wonderful. I read that the exhibition was shown only at the Art Institute, which held the largest collection of Monet's work outside of Paris and Boston. At the time, this exhibition is a comprehensive representation of Monet's career and the largest exhibition devoted to the artist; it aimed to include the best pieces from every period of Monet's working life."

"Yes, I read that article, too. It included something like one hundred fifty-nine works from around the globe, both from museums and private collections. Sixty-six institutions and thirty-seven private collections contributed paintings to the exhibition. Some highlights included the rarely loaned water-lily triptych from the museum of Modern Art, New York; The Carnegie Museum of Art's Water Lily Garden; seven of the Houses of Parliament Series done during the artist's stay in London; and the central panel of Luncheon on the Grass, which had never been exhibited outside Europe. The exhibition was extremely popular and exceeded museum projections with close to a million visitors."

"Well, it's settled then. I'll call the museum and find out the times they are showing today. I have a good friend who works in admissions, and I will try to get tickets from her."

After calling, Charlotte secured a reservation to be at the museum at 1:30 p.m. "Let's eat breakfast and then rest for a while before we get ready to go. My contact said that we must allow at least two hours for the exhibit. The one hundred fifty-nine paintings and drawings include many from private collections that are being shown for the first time and may never be again."

Heather nodded with a smile. "I am especially looking forward to seeing Monet's *Woman with a Parasol - Madame Monet and Her Son,* 1875."

After a short rest, the museum-going-pair arrived at the Art Institute of Chicago and received their tickets and museum guide. They made their way from room to room with many *ahs* and *oh, my Gods* until they reached Heather's favorite painting. She read from the museum's guide.

"With Manet's assistance, Monet found lodging in suburban Argenteuil in late 1871, a move that initiated one of the most fertile phases of his career. Impressionism evolved in the late 1860s from a desire to create full–scale, multi–figure depictions of ordinary people in casual outdoor situations. At its purest, impressionism was attuned to landscape painting, a subject Monet favored. In *Woman with a Parasol – Madame Monet and Her Son,* his skill as a figure painter is equally evident. Contrary to the artificial conventions of academic portraiture, Monet delineated the features of his sitters as freely as their surroundings. The spontaneity and naturalness of the resulting image were praised when it appeared in the second impressionist exhibition in 1876.

"*Woman with a Parasol* was painted outdoors, probably in a single session of several hours' duration. The artist intended the work to convey the feeling of a casual family outing rather than a formal portrait and used pose and placement to suggest that his wife and son interrupted their stroll while he captured their likenesses. The brevity of the moment portrayed here is conveyed by a repertory of animated brushstrokes of vibrant color, hallmarks of the style Monet was instrumental in forming. Bright sunlight shines from behind Camille to whiten the top of her parasol and the flowing cloth at her back, while colored reflections from the wildflowers below touch her front with yellow."

"You are right, this painting is incredible," said Charlotte. "Great idea to come here today. The exhibit will be leaving in three days."

"Yes. I just love Camille and the setting is idyllic. Imagine being her. Proud. Beautiful."

They made their way through the rest of the exhibit and were exhausted by the time they finished. They hailed a cab and rode home. Once inside the apartment, they quickly undressed and headed to bed for a nap.

Once awake, they regretted their idyllic weekend was coming to a close and they would have to get back to the jury and work tomorrow.

"I had a wonderful weekend and I'm so glad that we connected with each other," Charlotte shared with Heather as they hugged like they were never going to let go.

"I agree," Heather whispered.

Charlotte headed to the refrigerator and took out leftovers for "their last meal" for a while. Food finished and dishes in the sink, the tired lovers headed for bed and sleep.

The alarm rang.

"It's time to get up," Charlotte said, turning off the alarm.

The lovers got dressed and were ready for the day. They had breakfast and got into their cars and went back to their reality, planning to meet again next week.

Chapter Forty-Nine

August 21, 1995, Trial

"Judge Simpson acknowledged that the Prosecution completed their case."

"Now, Mr. Huffington, you may call your witnesses."

"Thank you, Your Honor. I would like to call Yolanda Williams," said the defense attorney.

The bailiff swore this witness in. "Raise your right hand. Do you promise that the testimony you shall give in the case before this court shall be the truth, the whole truth, and nothing but the truth, so help you God?"

"I do."

"Ms. Williams, what relationship do you have with the defendant?"

"He is a friend."

"Yolanda Williams testified that allegedly she heard the defendant say, 'I don't have to worry no more. I took care of my problem.'"

"Wendy White is pissed at D'Quandree because he beat up her cousin, which left him in the ICU with life-threatening injuries. She'll say anything to diss D'Quandree. She is an evil bitch."

"Please watch your language," Huffington warned. "You may continue."

"She doesn't like D'Quandree and she will say anything to get to him."

"So, you are saying that the defendant didn't boast that he no longer had a problem because he took care of it?"

"That's right."

"Were you in the house when the defendant boasted that he no longer had a problem?"

"Yeah, I was there, and I didn't hear him say anything like that!"

"Okay, Your Honor, I am finished with this witness," Huffington said.

"Mr. Emerson, you may cross-examine," Judge Simpson offered.

"Ms. Williams, you say that the defendant didn't boast that he no longer had a problem?"

"Yes."

"Are you saying that Ms. White lied?"

"I don't know about that. I just know I didn't hear what she thought she heard."

"Did you hear the defendant boast about anything?"

"He was always shooting off his mouth about this and that to build himself up with his boys."

"Your Honor, no further questions for this witness."

"Your Honor, I'd like to call my next witness, Jasara Pope."

The bailiff swore this witness in. "Do you promise to tell the whole truth and nothing but the truth, so help you God?"

"I do."

"Ms. Pope, what is your relationship to the defendant?"

"I'm just a friend. I hang out with defendant and his homies. I chill with them."

"What were you doing on the evening of July 12, 1995?"

"I was in Leslie Smith's apartment. She is my cousin."

"Did you see the defendant that evening?"

"Yes, I did."

"Did you notice what clothes he was wearing?"

"Not sure. I don't remember what people are wearing."

"Was he wearing a black-hooded sweatshirt that night?"

"I can't say for sure, but I remember he was wearing a black indigo pullover shirt with a picture of 2Pac - Me Against The World."

"Well, I would say you remember more than what you say you can. No black-hooded sweatshirt?

"No."

"I am through with this witness, Your Honor."

"Mr. Emerson, you may cross-examine the witness," Judge Simpson said.

"Thank you, Your Honor."

"Ms. Pope, did you see the defendant in the morning or afternoon on August 21, 1995?"

"No, I didn't. I spent the day food shopping for my family."

"So, you would not know whether the defendant was wearing a black-hooded sweatshirt at all that day?"

"That's right. I didn't see him until the evening."

"Thank you, Ms. Pope. You may step down."

"Your Honor, I would like to call Aaron Jackson," the defendant's attorney said.

"Raise your right hand. Do you promise that the testimony you shall give in the case before this court shall be the truth, the whole truth, and nothing but the truth, so help you God?"

"I do."

"Mr. Jackson, what is your relationship with the defendant?"

"Well, we like to chill or hit the clubs. You know. Have fun."

"What were you doing on July 12, 1995, when the Attorney General was murdered?"

"Ree and I spent most of the day at my house. We were checking out the movies on TV."

"Were you with him in the evening, too?"

"Yeah, I spent most of the day with him."

"Was there any time that the defendant was not with you? Did he leave your apartment for any length of time?

"I think he was with me most of the afternoon and part of the evening."

"Did he leave at all?

"I don't think he did."

"What time did he leave your apartment?"

"It had to be six or seven p.m."

"Thank you very much. I have no further questions for this witness, Your Honor."

"Mr. Emerson, you may cross-examine this witness."

"Thank you, Your Honor."

"So, Mr. Jackson, you said that the defendant was with you all afternoon until six or seven p.m.?

"Yes."

"And he did not leave your apartment at all?"

"Well, come to think of it, he did say that he had an appointment and left my apartment."

"Do you know what time he left?

"No, I don't."

"When he left, did he come back at all that night?

"No, he didn't. I didn't see him the rest of the night."

"I'm finished with this witness, Your Honor."

"You may step down."

"Mr. Huffington, you may call your next witness," Judge Simpson said.

"I'd like to call Laquana Brown to the stand."

"The bailiff swore this witness in. "Raise your right hand. Do you promise that the testimony you shall give in the case before this court shall be the truth, the whole truth, and nothing but the truth, so help you God?"

"Ms. Brown, where were you on July 12, 1995?"

"I was returning from work on my way home and I got off at Clinton Station."

"What time did you arrive at Clinton Station?"

"About 5:30 p.m. I was in the parking lot when I heard a couple of shots and I looked up in the direction of the shots. I saw a white man in a black-hooded sweatshirt running out of the parking lot."

"Did you get a good look at the man? Can you identify him?"

"No. He was moving too fast."

"Do you remember what clothes he was wearing?"

"Yeah, he had a black hoody."

"Anything else that you remember?"

"No."

"Thank you, Your Honor."

"Mr. Emerson, you may cross-examine," Judge Simpson said.

"Thank you, Your Honor. Ms. Brown, are you sure of the color of the skin of the man running away in the Clinton Station parking lot? He was a Caucasian?"

"Yeah, I'm sure."

"Thank you, Ms. Brown. You may step down."

"Your Honor, I would like to call Doctor Stanley McLeish, a special DNA expert."

"Raise your right hand. Do you promise that the testimony you shall give in the case before this court shall be the truth, the whole truth, and nothing but the truth, so help you God?"

"I do."

"Doctor McLeish, have you had a chance to review the findings from Brackdon Laboratories?

"I have."

"Do you agree with Doctor Jonas Spring's findings?"

"I don't."

"Please explain to the court why you do not agree with their results?"

"First of all, I challenge the use of Brackdon's database in two respects. First, he argues that the database produced unreliable match frequencies. His access to underlying documentation of their database was restricted by the laboratory and the limited sample he was permitted to review showed an unacceptable differential in probability distribution when compared with the Promega database. The database was also unreliable because Brackdon had not been published in a peer review journal. Second, the underlying data constituted potentially exculpatory evidence and the states purported withholding constitutes a failure to uphold the defendant's constitutional rights."

Promega provides complete solutions for analysis of forensic DNA samples by capillary electrophoresis (CE). These include reagents and kits for all steps in CE analysis workflows.

Products include preprocessing reagents for swabs and card punches prior to direct amplification of database samples, and DNA isolation systems for casework samples. We also provide the PowerQuant® System for accurate, human-specific DNA quantitation, and PowerPlex® Systems for STR amplification of Y-specific or autosomal DNA that meet global and regional database requirements. For sample analysis, the Spectrum family of CE instruments provides both low- and high-throughput sample processing options.

"What else do you have to say about Brackdon's DNA analysis results?"

"I can show you an exhibit that shows the statistical differences between the Brackdon and Promega databases at a single genetic location, THO1. Using statistical analysis of the allele distributions in the two databases, a 'chi square test pattern' determined the probability of the two databases being truly different at this location to be greater than ninety-nine percent.

"Thank you very much, Doctor McLeish."

Chapter Fifty

August 22, 1995, Judge Instructs the Jury

Judge Mary Simpson instructed the jury that "the evidence of the defendant's prior convictions was to be considered only on the question of his credibility, and for no other purpose." She further instructed the jury that "the subject matter of his convictions is irrelevant to this case, and you should not be inflamed by or affected by the fact that a particular person or persons were the subject matter of his convictions. You are not in any way to consider who the subject of those convictions may have been in determining any issue in this case."

"Members of the jury, you have heard all the testimony concerning this case. It is now up to you to determine the facts. You and you alone are the judges of the fact. Once you decide what facts the evidence proves, you must then apply the law as I give it to you to the facts as you find them.

(720 ILCS 5/9-1) (from Ch. 38, par. 9-1)

Sec. 9-1. First degree murder; death penalties; exceptions; separate hearings; proof; findings; appellate procedures; reversals.

(a) A person who kills an individual without lawful justification commits first degree murder if, in performing the acts which cause the death:

(1) he or she either intends to kill or do great bodily harm to that individual or another, or knows that such acts will cause death to that individual or another; or

(2) he or she knows that such acts create a strong probability of death or great bodily harm to that individual or another; or

(3) he or she, acting alone or with one or more participants, commits or attempts to commit a forcible felony other than second degree murder, and in the course of or in furtherance of such crime or flight therefrom, he or she or another participant causes the death of a person.

Judge Simpson gave the jury her deliberations. "Members of the jury, now it is time for me to instruct you about the law you must follow in deciding this case. I will start by explaining your duties and the general rules that apply in every criminal case. Then I will explain the elements of the crimes that the defendant is accused of committing. You may think of the "elements" of the crimes as the essential ingredients, or important parts, of the proof of the crimes. Then I will explain some rules that you must use in evaluating testimony and evidence. And last, I will explain the rules that you must follow during your deliberations in the jury room, and the possible verdicts that you may return. Please listen very carefully to everything I say.

"You have two main duties as jurors. The first one is to decide what the facts are from the evidence that you saw and heard here in court. Deciding what the facts are is your job, not mine, and nothing I have said or done during this trial was meant to influence your decision about the facts in any way.

"Your second job is to take the law that I give you, apply it to the facts, and decide if the government has proved the defendant guilty beyond a reasonable doubt. It is my job to instruct you about the law, and you are bound by the oath you took at the beginning of the trial to follow the instructions that I give you, even if you personally disagree with one or more of them. This includes the instructions that I gave you during the trial, and these instructions. All the instructions are important, and you should consider them together as a whole.

"No defendant has any obligation to present any evidence at all, or to prove to you in any way that he is innocent. It is up to the government to prove that he is guilty, and this burden stays on the government from start to finish. You must find the defendant not guilty unless the evidence convinces you beyond a reasonable doubt that he is guilty.

"The government must prove every element, that is— every important part—of the crimes charged 'beyond a reasonable doubt.'

"A 'reasonable' doubt is a fair, honest doubt growing out of the evidence or lack of evidence and based on reason and common sense. Ultimately, a 'reasonable doubt' would simply be a doubt that you find to be reasonable after you have carefully and thoughtfully examined and discussed the facts and circumstances present in this case.

"Proof 'beyond a reasonable doubt' does not mean proof that amounts to absolute certainty, or beyond all possible doubt. It does not mean proof "beyond a shadow of doubt," nor does it mean that the government must prove any fact or any crime with mathematical precision. Doubts that are merely imaginary, or that arise from nothing more than speculative possibilities, or that are based only on sympathy, prejudice or guessing are not "reasonable" doubts.

"In addition, the law does not require that every fact mentioned in the case be proved beyond a reasonable doubt. Rather, the law requires that enough facts be proved to convince you, beyond a reasonable doubt, that the crime was committed and that the defendant is guilty. If you are convinced that the government, through the evidence, has proved the defendant guilty beyond a reasonable doubt, then the proper verdict is 'guilty.' If you are not convinced, a "not guilty" verdict must be returned.

"The lawyers' statements and arguments are not evidence. They're questions and objections. The indictment is not evidence. My legal rulings are not evidence. And my comments and questions are not evidence. Do not speculate about what some witness might have said or what some exhibit might have shown. Such things not in evidence are not evidence, and you are bound by your oath not to let them influence your decision in any way.

"Make your decision based only on the evidence, as I have defined it here, and nothing else. You should use your common sense in weighing the evidence. Consider it in light of your everyday experience with people and events and give it whatever weight you believe it deserves. If your experience tells you that certain evidence reasonably leads to a conclusion, you are free to reach that conclusion.

"Now, we have already discussed the terms 'direct evidence' and 'circumstantial evidence.' Direct evidence is simply evidence like the testimony of any eyewitness which, if you believe it, directly proves a fact. If a witness testified that he saw someone walking across a field and you believed him, that would be direct evidence that such a thing had happened.

"Circumstantial evidence is simply a collection of circumstances that indirectly proves a fact. If a witness said that he saw fresh footprints in newly fallen snow, that would be circumstantial evidence from which you could conclude that someone had recently been walking there. Legally, there is no difference between direct and circumstantial evidence. The law does not say that one is necessarily any better evidence than the other. You should consider all the evidence, both direct and circumstantial, and give it whatever weight you believe it deserves.

"Part of your job as jurors is to decide how believable each witness was. This is your job, not mine. It is up to you to decide if a witness' testimony was believable and how much weight you think it deserves. You are free to believe everything that a witness said, or only part of it, or you can believe none of it at all, even if the witness has not been contradicted. But you should, of course, act reasonably and carefully in making these decisions.

"Let me suggest some things for you to consider in evaluating each witness' testimony.

"Ask yourself if the witness was able to clearly see or hear the events. Sometimes even an honest witness may not have been able to clearly see or hear what was happening and may make a mistake.

"Ask yourself how good the witness's memory seemed to be. Did the witness seem able to accurately remember what happened?

"Ask yourself if there was anything else that may have interfered with the witness' ability to perceive or remember the events.

"Ask yourself how the witness looked and acted while testifying. Did the witness seem honestly to be trying to tell you what happened? Or did the witness seem to be evasive, confused or even lying?

"Ask yourself if the witness had any relationship to either side of the case, or anything to gain or lose that might influence the witness' testimony. Ask yourself if the witness had any bias, or prejudice, or reason for testifying that might lead the witness to lie or to slant testimony in favor of one side or the other.

"Ask yourself if the witness testified inconsistently while on the witness stand, or if the witness said or did anything off the stand that is not consistent with what the witness said while testifying. If you think that the witness was inconsistent, ask yourself if this makes the witness' testimony less believable. Sometimes it may; other times, it may not. For example, you might consider whether the inconsistency was understandable or explainable. You might also ask yourself if it seemed like an insignificant or common mistake, or if it seemed to indicate a deliberate attempt to mislead.

"Finally, ask yourself how believable the witness' testimony was in light of all the other evidence. Was the witness' testimony supported or was it contradicted by other evidence that you found believable? If you think that a witness' testimony was contradicted by other evidence, keep in mind that people sometimes do forget things, and that even two honest people who witness the same event may not describe it exactly the same way.

"One more point about the witnesses. Sometimes jurors wonder if the number of witnesses who testified on a particular point, or on one side or the other, makes any difference. It does not. Do not make any decisions based only on the number of witnesses who testified. What is more important is how believable the witnesses were, and how much weight you think their testimony deserves. Concentrate on that, not the numbers."

Charlotte thought, *When is the judge going to end her instructions to the jury? I feel myself falling asleep and I have to remain alert.*

"There is one more general subject that I want to talk to you about before I begin explaining the elements of the crimes charged. The lawyers for both sides objected to some of the things that were said or done during the trial. Do not hold that against either side. The lawyers have a duty to object whenever they think that something is not permitted by the rules of evidence. Those rules are designed to make sure that both sides receive a fair trial.

"And do not interpret my rulings on their objections as any indication of how I think the case should be decided. My rulings were based on the rules of evidence, not on how I feel about the case. Remember that your decision must be based only on the evidence that you saw and heard here in court.

"That concludes the part of my instructions explaining your duties and the general rules that apply in every criminal case. In a moment, I will explain the significant elements of the crimes that the defendant is accused of committing. But before I do that, I want to emphasize that the defendant is only on trial for the crimes charged in the indictment. Your job is limited to deciding whether the government has proved each crime charged. Also keep in mind that whether anyone else should be prosecuted and convicted for this crime is not a proper matter for you to consider. The possible guilt of others is no defense to a criminal charge. Your job is to decide if the government has proved the defendant guilty. Do not let the possible guilt of others influence your decision in any way.

"In just a moment, the bailiff will take you to the jury room to consider your verdict. I appoint Charlotte Steele to be the forewoman and she will preside over your deliberations the way that a chairperson does at a meeting. It will be the forewoman's duty to sign the verdict form when you have agreed on a verdict. Whatever verdict you render must be unanimous. That is each and every person must agree on the same verdict. The bailiff will now escort you to the deliberation room."

"All Rise. Stand, please escort the Jury to deliberation room."

Chapter Fifty-One

August 21, 1995, Jury Deliberation

The jurors filed into the jury room to begin their deliberations. After everyone greeted each other. A nervous cloud filled the room, Charlotte Steele reminded the jury that "We should follow the judge's instructions about the law. We should respect each other's opinions and value the different viewpoints you each bring to the case. It is okay to change your mind. Show respect to the other jurors by looking at the person speaking. Do not be afraid to speak up and express your views. Listen to one another. Do not let yourself be bullied into changing your opinion, and do not bully anyone else. Do not rush into a verdict to save time. The people in this case deserve your complete attention and thoughtful consideration."

Charlotte Steele welcomed the jurors to the deliberation room. "Everyone go around the room and introduce themselves and talk about your feelings and what you think about the case. We should have our first vote after we have thoroughly discussed all of the evidence presented and witness testimonies."

Charlotte also reminded the jurors to make sure that they focus the deliberations on the evidence and the law.

"My name is Charlotte Steele and I am an investigative reporter and I have reported on how the climate change is causing the Arctic glaciers to melt in the Artic. Other issues have brought me around the world. This is going to be an important trial with the killing of the district attorney. We must make sure we are diligent in our deliberation. I am glad I am here."

Roberta Armstrong was a homemaker, with four "wonderful" children. She was 43 years old, five-foot-five, with a pleasant smile and sparkling personality, and wore a casual pantsuit. She was excited to be on her first jury. Her husband was a retired Army Sergeant First Class. "I am overwhelmed by all of the evidence and testimony, but I look to the rest of you to help me understand what we are doing."

Steven Spiel was a security guard for Embassy Security Group and was married with two children. He was 47 years old, and enjoyed the solitude of his work. He had a bald head and sported a full goatee. He loved riding his Harley on weekends. "I've seen a lot of shady characters in all my years in security and this one—D'Quandree Jones—looks like another one. The evidence looks pretty strong against him, but we will deliberate."

Sam Dickson was Vice President of First Chicago NBD Corporation and had been married for twenty-three years and had three children. He was six-foot-ten and was sharply dressed in a Men's Wearhouse gray pinstriped suit. He looked forward to coaching his kids' soccer teams in the fall. "In my business, I have to rely on the facts and that is what I will do in this case. We have a lot of evidence and witness testimony to discuss, and I reserve my judgment now."

L'Kadie Spencer, a twenty-four-year-old African American male who was in his first year of medical school at Rush Medical School and he was studying to be a hematologist. He has a high-top fade haircut. He wanted to help children with sickle-cell anemia. L'Kadie loved to play pickup basketball at his school wearing his Jordan Air sneakers. "This man got himself into a lot of trouble. I'll need help to understand how the DNA process works."

Amy Spelling was a twenty-one-year-old African American female who was supervisor of the front end at Dominick's. Amy attended Truman College nights and hoped to earn an Associate's Degree in healthcare. She was a quiet spoken woman and looked shyly at the other jurors as she spoke. "I'm glad I'm here and I will do the best that I can do."

"There is a lot of evidence, and I look forward to our deliberation. I know that we are under a lot of pressure to decide justice for the killing of an Attorney General, and I know we will do our best," said Oliver Preston, a 60-year-old retired auto worker. "I have been married for forty years and I have three grown children. They are living in other states, but we try to get together a few times each year."

Alicia Cumming was a twenty-nine-year-old African American female, who drove a bus for the Chicago Transit Authority. She was about six-foot tall and weighed about two hundred pounds. She was single. "I don't like this defendant. I see his type all the time on the buses. Tough guy. Loudmouth. Gotta beat down the little man. We'll see what the evidence says."

Anxious to speak, Philip Beach was a thirty-six-year-old teller for the American National Bank. He wore a short side-swept crew cut. "I can't wait to get into the deliberations. This is an interesting case with a lot of evidence. Looks like he did it, but I'll wait for the deliberations to take my vote." He was married with three children and loved to vacation in his RV with his family.

Albert Bunch was a fifty-two-year-old African American and was a thirty-year member

of the UAW in Chicago. He was single with four children. He wore a classic, timeless color combination and a very traditional three-piece suit. It would be ranked at the top if you want to categorize suits for going to a meeting. He worked fifty hours a week and "has no time to fool around." He supports his right to put him away for life."

Aditya Bakshi was a sixty-six-year-old retiree from India. He spent his life in computer systems and now loved his own time to be with his family. He wore a Dhoti garment, which is the traditional dress for Indian men. The dhoti is a long-unstitched garment, mostly five yards in length. The clothing is tied at the waist and ankles, with a knot at the waist. The dhoti is mostly paired with the kurta, the combination which is known as dhoti kurta in eastern India. He is married with one child. "We must give the defendant the benefit of the doubt and look at all of the evidence and witness testimony before we rush to judgement. I look forward to our deliberations."

Delilah Jones, no relation to D'Quandree Jones, was a forty-two-year-old African American female, and she was unemployed at this time. She was laid off from General Mills in February. She was wearing a classic linen shirtdress. She was single with two children, and she looked forward to the deliberation. This was her first trial as a juror.

"Thank you, everyone, for your introductions, Looks like we have a very diverse group, and I hope everyone remains nonjudgmental until our final vote. We will try to spend a reasonable amount of time considering the evidence and the law and listening to each other's opinions before we will feel more confident to take our first vote.

"We will first look at the crime scene and autopsy photos. They are pictures of Attorney General Alphonse Ferguson after he was shot twice in the face. They are gruesome and if anyone needs to take a break from viewing them, you will be able to do so. We saw them as they were presented by the prosecutor during the trial. So here they are." Charlotte started passing the photos around in each direction.

Roberta Armstrong took one look at the gunshot photos and almost threw up. Her breathing became difficult, and she said, "Oooooh, these are gross! I have never seen anything like this. The AG didn't stand a chance."

Roberta gazed at the photos and quickly handed them to Steven Spiel like hot potatoes. "Here, you look at these photos. They are gruesome."

"Looks like the AG got into his car and, as he turned to sit, was caught by surprise and was shot through his right eye twice. He didn't deserve something like this and was just doing his job to eradicate gang behavior in Chicago. Why do bad things happen to good people?" the broad-shouldered security guard asked.

Charlotte quickly interjected her warning. "We cannot prejudge innocence or guilt from these photos until we have seen all of the evidence."

The photos were passed to several jurors and Amy Spelling gasped as she viewed the photos. "I wish we didn't have to see these photos, but we must as jurors. We have a lot to discuss before we make a final determination in this case. I am going to wait until the end."

A few more jurors looked at the photos until everyone viewed them. Charlotte then asked the jurors to consider the witnesses and evidence.

"We will discuss what each witness said and then we will look at the DNA results. Let's begin with Melissa White. She was at her daughter's house and heard the defendant boast, 'I don't have to worry no more. I took care of my problem.' She also said that the defendant recounted how he hid and shot the AG.

"Any comments from anyone?" asked Charlotte.

"Yes, I do," answered Aditya Bakshi. "Ms. White was not in the same room as the defendant, and she said she recognized the voice of the defendant. But how could she be so sure? There was rap music blasting and people talking loudly. I am not sure that we can prove that the defendant actually said these words."

"Come on, we know it was him," Albert Bunch angrily spoke. "He did it and this was him speaking. I'm ready for a vote of guilt or innocence."

"Not so quickly, Mr. Bunch," Delilah Jones chimed in. "We have not gone over all of the evidence, and we have a way to go. We should vote once we are able to discuss all the witness testimony and DNA evidence. I am not ready to take a vote now."

"I agree," Oliver Preston said. "We have a long way to go. Let's continue our deliberations."

"It is time for us to complete our discussion today," said Charlotte. "We will pick up where we left off and continue tomorrow morning. Everyone, have a good evening and don't forget, we cannot discuss these deliberations with each other or anyone else."

Charlotte notified the bailiff that they were done with today's deliberations, and he allowed everyone to leave the jury room and head home for the evening.

As they filed out of the room, Philip Beach grabbed Charlotte's arm and he whispered in her ear. "Jones did it and you have to get this charade over fast!"

Charlotte ignored him and continued to head for the exit.

Chapter Fifty-Two

August 21, 1995, End of Day One of Deliberations

As she drove home, Charlotte thought, *This is going to be the most difficult thing I have ever done. I must make sure that all of the facts are deliberated, and I must give everyone the time they need to make their minds up before we take a final vote of guilt or innocence.*

Charlotte entered her apartment, locked the door, and placed her purse and keys on her table. She went to her bedroom, took off her blouse and bra and slipped into a Led Zeppelin T-shirt and gray sweatpants. She was then off to the kitchen and poured a glass of Quilceda Creek Cabernet Sauvignon 2016.

As she slowly sipped her first taste, she turned on Miles Davis' "Kind of Blue" and sunk into her living room couch.

She got her cell phone from her pocketbook and quickly dialed Heather's phone number. The phone rang five times until she heard Heather's soft, "Hello."

"Heather, how are you doing? How was your day? I miss you."

"Hey, girl, great to hear from you. Whatcha doing?"

"I just got home from court, and I figured it was about time we talked."

"You got that right. How was your day? I'm missing you. Let's get together next weekend. Okay? You want to come to my place?"

"I'd love that. Let's talk later in the week and make plans."

"Okay."

She closed her eyes and drifted into the evening, leaving her court deliberations farther and farther away.

A half hour passed, and the reporter/foreperson awoke, startled by the phone ringing only to find out it was a telemarketer. She thought it was time to get up and have supper. She took out the shrimp that she defrosted last night for her shrimp scampi dinner. Once cooked, she enjoyed her dinner with more wine.

Dinner eaten, she put the dishes in the dishwasher. Charlotte then watched *Gone With the Wind* until she couldn't keep her eyes open, and she got ready for bed and crashed.

Chapter Fifty-Three

August 22, 1995, Day Two of Deliberations

"All rise. This court is now in session." Judge Simpson entered the courtroom sat down behind the bench, and told everyone else to be seated. "We will continue the case of the state of Illinois versus D'Quandree Jones. The jury is dismissed to the jury room to continue your deliberations," said Judge Simpson.

Once in the jury room, Charlotte began the day's discussion with a review of the witness for the prosecution, Wendy White. "Ms. White said she saw the defendant soaking his hands in bleach at Leslie Smith's apartment and she wondered why he was doing this. She also noted that he was no longer wearing his black-hooded sweatshirt that he was wearing earlier in the day. She also heard the defendant say, "I have no more worries and I don't have a prosecutor."

"Who wants to start this discussion regarding Ms. White's testimony?" the forewoman asked.

Albert Bunch spoke up. "I will. Here's a woman who saw the defendant washing his hands in bleach. Come on, people. Why would someone do that? You know! He was trying to get the blood off his hands. Why else?"

"I can tell you the US Centers for Disease Control and Prevention explains how to mix bleach with water to clean your hands to minimize infection or clear it up," said Oliver Preston, retired auto worker. "I used to use the water-bleach solution, especially after a dirty engine repair."

"It is also used to prevent certain diseases," L'Kadie Spencer said, who was in his first year at Rush Medical School. "So, you see, there could be many reasons the defendant was washing his hands with bleach."

"I still feel the defendant was trying to remove the AG's blood and you cannot tell me anything else," Bunch said defiantly.

"We also have the issue of the black-hooded sweatshirt," Roberta Armstrong added. "Ms. White noted that the defendant was no longer wearing his black-hooded sweatshirt at night. This would be significant since a black-hooded sweatshirt was found near the crime scene."

"Ya, but," Bunch responded, "like Clarence Huffington asked her when she said this. 'Since when do you notice what people are wearing?'"

"Any other discussion on this witness? Charlotte asked. "None? We will move on.

The next witness is Harold Haynes. Who remembers what he said?"

Sam Dickson was the next juror to respond. "Harold Haynes said that the defendant recounted how he shot the AG. He also told him not to snitch. I believe that Haynes is telling the truth, and the defendant did shoot the AG."

"Let's not jump to conclusions over this testimony," Aditya Bakshi, the retiree from India, said. "Even though Mr. Haynes reported this, it doesn't mean that the defendant did this crime. Gangbangers like the defendant like to brag, and maybe that is what he was doing."

"Let's move on to the testimony of Snake Eyes Washington," Charlotte said. "We must keep on track with these deliberations, and we cannot make any determinations at this point in the deliberations. We have much more to discuss."

"Let's see. Snake Eyes Washington said he took the defendant to Union Station to meet a friend," Delilah Jones said. "I later recognized Alphonse Ferguson from television reports about the murder as the man whom Jones asked him to follow."

She also stated that Washington asked the defendant the day after the murder if he did it. The defendant told him, "Don't worry about it, don't say fuckin' nothing and if anyone asks, I never asked you to follow Ferguson and never say anything about it."

"I think that Washington probably brought and picked up the defendant after the murder of the AG. After all, he was told to follow the AG on the train to where he got off."

"Sounds like we have more evidence that the defendant is guilty of the murder of Alphonse Ferguson, the Attorney General," added Steven Spiel, security guard. "Again, the evidence is mounting against the defendant."

"It sure is," Alicia Cumming said with confidence. "If it walks like a duck and quacks like a duck. It is a duck. He is guilty."

"Okay, we are getting ahead of ourselves," the forewoman chimed in. "We have a lot more to discuss, and let's call it a day."

The jurors filed out of the room briskly and headed for the exit to go home.

Clarence Huffington met with D'Quandree Jones at the latter's request.

"The fucking jury is deliberating," blasted Jones. "Do you know what they are talking about? How long is this going to go on?"

"We don't have any idea how the deliberations are progressing. We won't know until they are ready to make a verdict in your case," Huffington answered.

"How long must I be locked up? It is time for me to go home. I have had enough of this isolation. I want to go back home. Do you know how long this is going to drag on?"

"I have no idea. It is up to the jury at this point. You will know once you are called to court and hear the verdict."

"I pay you a fuckin' bundle. You gotta get me out of here!"

Chapter Fifty-Four

August 23, 1995, Day Three of Deliberations

"Welcome back, everyone," the forewoman said. "I hope you all had a good evening's sleep. We have a lot of business to deal with. We still have a long way to go. We will take our first vote of guilt or innocence once we have discussed all of the witness testimonies just to get an idea of where we stand as a jury."

"We will begin our deliberations today with Ralph Davis. He was the gentleman who parked near Alphonse Ferguson, the Attorney General, at the Clinton Station parking lot and saw a figure bend over into the car and shoot the AG. Although Mr. Davis could not ID the shooter, it was important to know that the shooting was witnessed. Anyone else?"

"Well, according to Mr. Davis, the shooter was wearing a black-hooded sweatshirt," Oliver Preston said. "At least we know the shooter was wearing this sweatshirt, and another witness remembered that he was not wearing it the day of the murder. The sweatshirt was found along the tracks with other pieces of clothing that provided DNA evidence that the defendant was at the shooting."

"I have to agree with Mr. Preston," Alicia Cumming said. "It had to be the defendant. He was wearing a black-hooded sweatshirt and later that day, Ms. White observed that he no longer was wearing it. I know he did it. The defendant is a punk. Just look at him with that blank stare. He did it. I don't have to wait any further to vote," expressed the bus driver.

"I don't have to remind all of you again that we have to wait until all of the witness testimony is gone over before we take our first vote," Charlotte said. "Now we'll discuss the DNA testing and results."

"The DNA was tested by three laboratories. The first was Brackdon Laboratories, and the testimony was given by their former director, Doctor Jonas Spring. They were given a black-hooded sweatshirt, a pair of gloves, a knit cap, and a yellow bandana. Doctor Spring reported that Ferguson's DNA was a match at six different genetic markers on all of the garments.

"Once they discovered Ferguson's DNA was present on some of the garments found at the crime scene, they also tested to determine who wore these garments. They investigated 'friction areas' and once they received D'Quandree Jones's blood sample, they were able to determine that Jones could not be excluded as a donor for the samples recovered. Any thoughts?"

"I believe in the facts of the case to help me make a determination of guilt or innocence," articulated the nicely dressed VP, Sam Dickson. "So, we are beginning to see a pattern here of guilt. The defendant's clothing has Ferguson's DNA. I wonder how it got there. And we have witnesses telling us how the defendant bragged about the elimination of the AG. I feel we can close up shop now."

"I have to agree with Sam," Steven Spiel sounded off. "I think we should take our first vote of guilt or innocence. What do you think, Ms. Forewoman?"

"Well, let's see a raise of hands in favor of a vote," Charlotte answered.

At first, everyone just sat there, and then little by little hands started raising.

"Looks like we have eight hands for a vote and four against. Looks like the majority is in favor of a vote. Let me ask the bailiff for some paper that we can use for our vote, since our votes will be secret ballots."

Charlotte left the room and returned with paper and pens. "Okay, each take a piece of paper and a pen and mark your ballot, guilty or not guilty. Once you vote, I'll come around the room and collect the ballots."

Charlotte collected the ballots and began counting the ballots and shielded them from the other jurors. "All right, we have six votes for 'guilty,' four votes for 'not guilty' and two were undecided.

"All right, let's get back to the deliberations. We can now discuss DNA laboratory, #2, the FBI. Keith Anderson, Deputy Special Agent testified that the DNA pattern for the bandana matched Ferguson. He also said they were able to prove that Jones was a potential donor on the black-hooded sweatshirt and the defendant could not be excluded as a donor on the collar of the sweatshirt. Any discussion?"

"I think this DNA is junk science," said Alicia Cumming, "but the AG's blood was on the defendant's sweatshirt and that must mean something."

Delilah Jones stated that this was her first introduction to DNA, but she heard it is being used more in trials. "I read that many criminals have been found innocent after spending years in jail because their DNA could not be found at the crime scene. Here we have a defendant whose sweatshirt has evidence of the AG's blood. The AG was shot at close range. This could be the defendant."

"Anything else on the FBI's findings? Nothing? Okay we will move on to the third laboratory, DNA Diagnostics Center. Who remembers what evidence they found?"

Aditya Bakshi spoke up. "They were able to say that the defendant's DNA was found on the collar of the black-hooded sweatshirt from a friction area where the defendant's skin cells were transferred to the sweatshirt. Also, it was shown in earlier testimony that the AG's DNA was found on the sweatshirt."

"We've been through a lot today," the forewoman said. "Let's call it a day. Have a good evening, everyone, and please do not discuss this case with each other or anyone else."

The bailiff was notified that deliberations were over today and opened the jury door and the jurors left the courthouse and went home.

Chapter Fifty-Five

August 24, 1995, Day Four of Deliberations

The jury arrived for their deliberations but was told to remain in the courtroom. A surprise witness was called by the prosecution, and he was sworn in by the bailiff.

The bailiff swore this witness in. "Raise your right hand. Do you promise that the testimony you shall give in the case before this court shall be the truth, the whole truth, and nothing but the truth, so help you God?"

Prosecutor Ralph Emerson stood up. "Your Honor, we have a special situation in this trial, and I would like to question our special witness."

"What is your name?

"People call me Uncle Freddie," the country drifter responded.

"What is your occupation?"

"I am happily retired, and I drive and stop at rest stops along the way and meet some wonderful people. I share my collection of valuable books, games, pictures with anyone who stops and talks with me."

"Where were you on July 12, 1995?"

"I stopped to rest in the parking lot of the Clinton Station in Chicago."

"Please tell the court what you witnessed on that day."

"I saw this guy come to his car, and he opened the driver's door and started to sit behind the steering wheel when another man whipped open the door and yelled something and then shot the driver twice. He ran from that car out of the parking lot."

"Did you see who did the shooting?

"Yes."

"Is he in this courtroom?"

"There he is over there," he said, pointing to the defendant.

"Are you sure he is the person who shot the driver of that car?"

"He is."

"Why didn't you tell someone about this before?"

"As I said, I am a drifter all over the country. I just recently saw that man's face on TV as the possible shooter of the Attorney General. When I saw what happened, I called the police and told them what I know and here I am."

"Well, thank you very much, Uncle Freddie. Your Honor, I don't have anything else for this witness," exclaimed the smiling prosecutor.

"Mr. Huffington, do you have any questions for this witness?" asked Judge Simpson.

"You bet I do, Your Honor," announced the defense attorney.

"Uncle Freddie, here we are at the end of the trial, and you show up like Superman with a damning exclamation that you saw the defendant shoot the AG. How do you know it was him?"

"All I know, I was minding my own business by my car, and I heard this dude yell and then lean into a car and shoot someone."

"How far away from the car where you were minding your own business?"

"I would say just about the same distance where the defendant is sitting."

"Did you see his face?

"Yes, I did, as he got up from shooting and turned to leave the parking lot."

"Do you drink alcohol or use drugs, Uncle Freddie?"

"I don't do either. I love life just the way it is. I don't need to get any higher than I already am."

"Are you depressed, or have you ever been hospitalized for depression?

"No."

Judge Simpson told Uncle Freedie to step down.

"Your Honor, can we approach?"

"Yes, approach the bench," Judge Simpson ordered.

"Your Honor, here we are, and the trial is almost over, and we have this drifter coming forward to tell us that he witnessed the shooting of the Attorney General. Years later, he remembers seeing the defendant in the Clinton Station parking lot shooting the Attorney General. I question his credibility," Huffington stated.

"I could see something like this happening," said the prosecutor, who was feeling confident at this point. "He is a traveler and didn't see anything about this crime until he recently watched TV. He wants to do what is right, and he came forward. He has nothing to prove."

"Gentlemen, I'm going to allow his testimony. He witnessed the crime and is sharing that with us now. I will allow his testimony. You may return to your seats.

"Members of the jury, we are going to allow Uncle Freddie's testimony in the record, and you may return to your room and continue your deliberations," advised Judge Simpson.

The jury returned to their room and, once everyone was seated, Charlotte addressed the group. "Well, this is an eye-opener. Looks like the case just took a turn in a different direction. Discussion?" asked the surprised forewoman.

"I knew it!" exclaimed Alicia Cumming. "I knew It. I knew he did it. This testimony wraps things up for me. Those of you who thought he was innocent, this is a wake-up call for you. You need to change your vote."

"I have to agree with you, Alicia," chimed in Steven Spiel. Several jurors nodded in agreement.

"We should probably take another vote now," added L'Kadie Spencer.

"Okay we will," said Charlotte. "I'll pass out the paper and pens again and please write your vote on the ballot, and I will go around and collect them once everyone is done."

The jurors didn't take long to register their votes. Charlotte collected the votes and started counting. "We have one, two, three, four votes for guilty. Looks like we have eleven votes guilty and one not guilty."

"What the fuck!" yelled a few of the jurors. "What can we do to help change the one 'not guilty?'"

"Let me address the 'not guilty' person," Albert Bunch said. "What more do you need to see that this defendant did the crime? The DNA showed he was at the shooting. We have witnesses who recounted the boasting of the defendant that he no longer had a problem. And now we have a witness who saw the defendant shoot the AG. Come on, man!"

"I have to agree with you Albert," Philip Beach verbalized. "It is obvious the defendant is guilty considering all of the evidence and now we have an eyewitness to the crime. What do we need to do to bring this non-believer to our side? I know this is a secret ballot, but I'd love to know who cannot see the light."

"Okay, let's come back to do what we should do, and that is deliberate," broadcasted the capable forewoman. "We came here to deliberate, and that is what we will continue to do. Everyone deserves their own opinion, and we shall see if we can all agree on one verdict."

"Anyone have any ideas on how we can turn this around? asked Charlotte.

"Well, we could do a quick review of all the witness testimony and evidence, if that helps," offered Oliver Preston.

"What does the group think about that suggestion?" asked Charlotte. "Let's go around the room for any other suggestions."

Roberta Armstrong went first and agreed that might be a good idea to review everything.

Charlotte then asked the group, "Show a raise of hands if you want a review of everything before we take another vote."

"Okay, all of your hands went up, so we will go through the evidence presented and hopefully it will make a difference in our vote."

Methodically, Charlotte went over the evidence. She allowed the discussion to understand what was provided to the jurors. Once all of the evidence and witness testimonies were reviewed, Charlotte asked everyone to raise their hand if they were ready to vote guilty or not guilty. All of the hands went up.

"Okay, we will now vote by secret ballot." The jurors checked guilty or not guilty on the slips of paper provided by the Bailiff.

Charlotte announced each vote, and it was a consensus, twelve to zero. Everyone voted "guilty." The jurors felt a sense of relief. Now their duty was over.

Chapter Fifty-Six

August 25, 1995—The Verdict

When the jury returned to the courtroom, Judge Simpson asked, "Have you reached a verdict?"

Charlotte Steele, Jury Foreperson, stood. "We have, Your Honor."

"What say you?"

"With respect to first-degree murder, we, the jury, find the defendant guilty."

After hearing the verdict, Judge Simpson asked the foreperson of the jury if the verdict was correct—if that was what the jury unanimously decided, Absent from the verdict was a sentence that would be determined later by the judge, should the verdict be guilty.

"It is."

"Thank you, jury, for your service today."

Jones' reputation for violence and vengeance created an atmosphere of tension throughout the trial. The court had sharply curtailed camera coverage, and the judge excused two jurors just before the start of the trial after they expressed fear for their safety.

The newspaper further reported that the case against Jones consisted of testimony from some of Jones' former gang allies and from two women who said they had heard him boast about the crime. Another witness testified that she saw Jones near the scene of the crime around the time of the murder.

In addition, experts testified that Jones' DNA profile was found on clothes left behind on railroad tracks near the murder scene. Jones' defense lawyers had argued that DNA testing was flawed and that those gang associates were under intense pressure from the police to implicate Jones in the murder.

Jones shook his head and slumped in his chair when the verdict was announced Saturday afternoon. Court bailiffs shackled him and the judge ordered him to remain in the courtroom while Alphonse Ferguson's eighty-five-year-old father, Edward Ferguson, read an eloquent impact statement from the witness stand.

"About a month before my son's murder, I had suggested to him that he might want to consider leaving state service for more lucrative opportunities in the private practice of law. He looked at me and said, 'Not yet, Dad. I still think, in time, I can make a difference.'"

Just then, Snake Eyes and Washington grabbed the AR-15s that were taped under their chairs and opened fire, shouting, "You die!"

Four rows behind D'Quandree Jones, Snake Eyes sprayed bullets around the courtroom. A bullet struck Jones in the middle of his head, killing him instantly as he slumped to the desk, face-down. He never knew what hit him. Snake Eye's array of ammunition also hit and instantly killed Jones' attorney, the court reporter, and Judge Simpson.

Simultaneously, Washington killed both the prosecution attorneys and a bailiff and wounded some jurors.

The courtroom was a battle scene. It was pure pandemonium, as people were screaming, crying, and running for cover. Most rushed for the exit, knocking each other down and trampling some amid the chaos.

The shooters successfully hit their targets before court officers rushed the courtroom after hearing shots fired and shot them down, killing them.

Once their threat was over, first responders rushed from one victim to the next and rushed the wounded out of the courtroom to the ambulances waiting outside.

A few of the court officers were wounded as were a few members of the jury. Charlotte Steele fell to the floor, with blood spurting from her right arm and right shoulder.

Jones got his wish. He doesn't have to rot in a prison cell.

About the Author

E.A. Kellner lives in Myrtle Beach with his wife, Alice, and Dylan the dog. He has eighteen grandchildren and six great-grandchildren (don't ask him their birth dates). He loves writing daily and is currently working on an autobiography. He picked up golf after an absence of fifty years and they live on the fourteenth hole of a local course. He has a season pass to play miniature golf with his buddies. He loves to go to the beach with his wife, although they are relegated to sitting on the water's edge and are unable to advance further in the water. They like to take day rides to nowhere and can frequently be found browsing in antique shops.

* 9 7 9 8 8 6 8 9 1 8 5 6 8 *